THE WIZARD
AND THE
WITCH

Jean Ure
Illustrations by David Anstey

WALKER BOOKS
AND SUBSIDIARIES
LONDON • BOSTON • SYDNEY

For my own Furry Walloper
(Witch by courtesy of husband)

First published 1995 by Walker Books Ltd
87 Vauxhall Walk, London SE11 5HJ

This edition published 1995

2 4 6 8 10 9 7 5 3 1

Text © 1995 Jean Ure
Illustrations © 1995 David Anstey
Cover illustration © 1995 Julek Heller

The right of Jean Ure to be identified as author
of this work has been asserted by her in accordance with the
Copyright, Designs and Patents Act 1988.

This book has been typeset in Sabon.

Printed in England

British Library Cataloguing in Publication Data
A catalogue record for this book
is available from the British Library.

ISBN 0-7445-4303-7

CONTENTS

Chapter One

The twins and Primple – Primple was their dog – were playing Goodies and Baddies at the bottom of the garden. Gemma was being a Baddie, with a handkerchief mask tied over her face. Joel, as a Goodie, was just about to throw her to the ground and sit on her when all of a sudden there was a terrible screeching and the sky overhead turned black as midnight.

"What is it?" whispered Gemma, peering out from behind the tree where she had been hiding.

"I don't know." Joel stopped, and looked up. So did Primple.

As the darkness cleared, they saw a hunched shape astride a broomstick. It was making straight for them, red eyes gleaming and pointed teeth bared, cackling as it came.

"It's a witch!" yelled Joel. "Run for it!"

Pell mell up the garden raced the twins, Primple hot on their heels. (He wasn't a very brave dog, but then he was only tiny.) The broomstick came after them. Hideous shrieks filled the air.

"Quick!" panted Joel.

The twins and Primple pounded up the path. Could they manage to reach the house before the broomstick overtook them?

Joel reached it; Gemma reached it. Poor Primple, with his stubby legs, took a desperate leap at the kitchen doorstep, missed his footing and went tumbling backwards, head over heels. At that moment, the witch struck. Zooming in on a steep nosedive, she seized a squealing Primple by the scruff of his neck and shot triumphantly upwards, screaming with unearthly laughter.

Gemma, in despair, cried, *"Primple!"*

Joel tore back into the garden. He shook his fist at the departing broomstick.

"Hey, you! You give us our dog back!"

He snatched up a large stone from the rockery and threw it, but the broomstick was already out of reach, circling the chimney pots.

"Primple!" wept Gemma. "Oh, Primple!"

And then, just as Joel was about to run to the top of the rockery and shout swear words, the broomstick completed one final lap of the chimney pots and swept in, very smoothly, to land.

"Ha ha! Fooled you that time!"

The witch had disappeared. In her place, very jaunty and full of himself, sat a small grinning wizard in a green cloak. On his shoulder, seemingly none the worse for his adventure, sat Primple, lovingly nibbling his ear.

"Oh, it's you!" Gemma was half relieved, half indignant. She might have known it: Ben-Muzzy, their wizard friend, playing stupid pranks.

"Did you think I was a real witch?" said Ben-Muzzy, plainly very pleased with himself.

"Not really," said Joel. "I pretty soon guessed it was you."

"Well, I didn't!" said Gemma, who on the whole was more truthful than her twin. She gathered Primple tenderly into her arms. "Imagine if you'd dropped him! Poor little man, he must have been terrified."

"Does he look terrified?" said Ben-Muzzy.

Gemma had to admit that he didn't. Primple liked Ben-Muzzy. In fact, it had been Ben-Muzzy who had magicked him out of a hat in the first place (which was the reason that Primple was pale pink with blue spots: Ben-Muzzy's magic didn't always turn out quite right).

"He enjoyed it," said Ben-Muzzy.

"It still wasn't very responsible," grumbled Gemma.

"It wasn't meant to be responsible! It's All Spells' Night. Wizards do that sort of thing on All Spells' Night."

"What, go round frightening people?"

"Cast spells and play tricks."

"Well, I think it was a very silly trick," said Gemma. "Very *childish*."

Ben-Muzzy sulked. He aimed a kick at the broomstick.

"Just because you haven't any sense of humour," he muttered.

"I've got a sense of humour! When things are *funny*. How would you like it if Podnock had played the same trick on you?"

Podnock was another wizard. He and Ben-Muzzy both worked for a master wizard called Wollibar. They were always playing practical jokes on each other.

"As a matter of fact – " Ben-Muzzy announced it with dignity – "Podnock and a gang of others have turned themselves into black cats for the night. I could have gone with them, had I wanted, but I thought I'd come and see you, instead. I thought," said Ben-Muzzy, "that you'd be pleased to see me."

"Well, I would have been," said Gemma, "if you'd just arrived on the broomstick in the normal way."

"What about Wollibar?" said Joel. "Does he know you've pinched his broomstick?"

"No; I magicked another in its place. It won't fly, but it looks the same."

"Hope he doesn't want to use it," said Joel.

"Not on All Spells' Night. All the masters and the grand highs stay home by their cauldrons while we play Spell-or-Spill."

"What's Spell-or-Spill?"

"If they don't let us play a trick on them we upset their cauldrons."

"*Honestly,*" said Gemma.

"They're only little tricks," pleaded Ben-Muzzy.

"I didn't think it was a very little trick that you just played on us."

Ben-Muzzy looked at Joel. Joel looked at Ben-Muzzy. They rolled their eyes. There were times when Gemma did keep on.

"I *had* thought," said Ben-Muzzy, "that we might all go off together and have some fun."

"I wouldn't mind." Joel was always ready for a bit of fun, especially with Ben-Muzzy. Ben-Muzzy's spells might not always be quite reliable, and sometimes they did have rather unpleasant results, like the time he had turned Joel into a caterpillar and couldn't turn him back again, but at least it was never boring. Playing Goodies and Baddies with Gemma was tame in comparison.

"I'll tell you what!" said Joel, suddenly growing excited. "I'll tell you *what*! We could go and be witches in Graham Foster's garden and give him a fright!"

"Good idea," said Ben-Muzzy. "Who's Graham Foster?"

"He's a nerd," said Joel. "He broke a glass at school the other day and wouldn't own up, and it was me that got the blame."

"Well, it was mostly your fault," pointed out Gemma. "You pushed him."

"Only because he tried to trip me up."

"Only because you called him names."

"Only because he deserved it!"

Gemma sniffed.

"Where does he live?" said Ben-Muzzy. "This nerd?"

"Just over there." Joel flapped a hand. "Turn me into a witch and I'll show you!"

"I'll turn you into a witch when we get there. We don't want to attract attention."

"All right," said Joel. "When we get there."

Gemma looked at them, pityingly. Did they think that one wizard and a pair of twins riding on a broomstick weren't likely to attract attention?

"On you get!" said Ben-Muzzy.

Joel hopped astride. He glanced back at his twin.

"Are you coming, or not?"

Gemma hesitated. "What are you going to do after you've frightened Graham Foster?"

"Hah! Well, I have been dared," said Ben-Muzzy, "to go and play a trick on a *real* witch."

"Play a trick on a real witch?" said Gemma. "Isn't that rather dangerous?"

Ben-Muzzy sniggered. "Not if it's this particular witch!"

"Which particular witch?" said Joel.

"This particular witch that's completely

loopy and messes up on all her spells. They got so sick of her always turning people into roads when she meant toads and causing plagues of hats instead of rats that they chucked her out. Now she's sulking all by herself in a cave."

"And you want to go and play tricks on her?" said Gemma.

"I have been *dared*," said Ben-Muzzy.

"Who by?"

"Podnock. Last All Spells' Night he and some friends went flying over on the broomstick and shouted rude things at her –"

"What sort of rude things?"

"Oh, just anything that occurred to them … stupid old witch, can't get her spells right. That sort of thing. And then they dropped stuff into her cauldron, bits of twig and stuff – "

"Why?" said Gemma. "What did they do that for?"

"For fun," said Ben-Muzzy.

Gemma looked at him, rather hard.

"Anyway – " Ben-Muzzy turned, hastily, to Joel – "Podnock's dared me to fly over and do the same, so that's where I'm going after we've frightened your friend the nerd."

"I'll come with you!" said Joel.

"Playing tricks on some poor old witch that's been chucked out … I think that's mean," said Gemma.

"I don't," said Joel. "I think it's brilliant! Anyone that turns people into roads jolly well deserves to have tricks played on them."

"Serve you right if she turned you into a road," said Gemma.

Joel turned his back on her. There were times when he grew just a little bit sick of his twin always being so superior. "Let's go!" he shouted.

"Hang about!" said Gemma. "Hang about! I haven't said yet whether I'm coming or not."

"Don't want you," said Joel.

"It's not up to you, it's up to Ben-Muzzy!"

"He doesn't want you, either. Do you?" said Joel, prodding at him.

"Um … well. I wouldn't say that, exactly."

Ben-Muzzy was cautious. He *had* been known to get into scrapes when he went off on his adventures, and Gemma was a useful person to have around if you were in a scrape. She was of a more practical turn of mind than her twin.

"Well, get on, then, if you must!" roared Joel.

"What about Primple?"

"We can't take him with us."

Gemma bristled. "Why not?"

"Can't take a *dog*."

"He's quite right," said Ben-Muzzy. "Dogs are nothing but a nuisance on a broomstick."

"Funny he wasn't a nuisance just now," said Gemma. "Funny that you seemed to *like* him on the broomstick just now."

"Why don't you go and put a bag over your head?" said Joel. He'd had enough of Gemma wittering on. He wanted to get off and frighten Graham Foster.

Gemma stuck out her lower lip. She could be stubborn when she wanted.

"If *we're* having fun, I don't see why Primple can't. Why should he be left out?"

"Because he'd fall off," said Ben-Muzzy.

"Oh. All right, then. Why didn't you say? Poor little man! We wouldn't want you falling off, *would* we?"

Gemma tucked Primple under her arm and carried him back indoors. Ben-Muzzy looked at Joel, slightly shamefaced.

"He wouldn't really fall off. Nothing can

fall off a broomstick once it's in flight. But dogs don't understand about broomsticks the way cats do. Cats sit still; dogs bounce about. Then the broomstick gets unstable. She wouldn't like that."

"No, she'd start moaning that she felt sick. She always gets sick. Every time we go anywhere in the car we have to keep stopping so she can get out."

"Yes, and we wouldn't want to keep stopping on the broomstick," said Ben-Muzzy. "You'd never know where you were going to land."

"So it's just as well," said Joel, as his twin came back.

"What's just as well?" demanded Gemma.

"Nothing to do with you," said Joel. "Can we go now?"

Gemma hesitated.

"I've just had another thought."

Joel and Ben-Muzzy groaned.

"What now?" said Joel.

"Shouldn't we tell Mum where we're going?"

"Oh, yes, that's a great idea," said Joel, heavily sarcastic. "Let's tell her … we're just going to fly off on a broomstick and play tricks on people... That's really great, that is! She'd really go for that."

"But she'll wonder where we are," protested Gemma. "And it's going to be dark soon."

"Tell her we're going to see Graham Foster, because we *are*," said Joel.

Gemma looked at him, doubtfully. It wasn't quite a lie – but almost as good as.

"Wait!" Ben-Muzzy stepped off the broomstick. He took his tall wizard's hat from his head and flung it majestically into the air, solemnly chanting as he did so:

"While we are away,
Let it stay day.
By wizard's will,
Let time stand still."

The hat reappeared on Ben-Muzzy's head.

"There you are," said Ben-Muzzy. "She won't even know that you've gone."

"Brilliant!" breathed Gemma.

"*Now* can we go?" said Joel.

Gemma jumped on to the broomstick behind him.

"What did you say the name of your friend

was?" asked Ben-Muzzy.

"He's not a friend," said Joel, "he's a nerd and his name's Graham Foster."

"Graham Foster." Ben-Muzzy began muttering to himself. To fly a broomstick you had to talk to it in special broomstick talk – in other words, backwards. Ben-Muzzy was getting better at it, but he wasn't really what you would call fluent.

"Retsof – Maharg – ot – su – ekat!"

The broomstick slowly tilted its nose into the air.

"We're off!" said Gemma.

At last, thought Joel.

Chapter Two

There was only one problem with flying over the town on a broomstick: people kept stopping to point and stare as if they couldn't believe their eyes, which most probably they couldn't.

"Look at them!" cried Joel, leaning dangerously over the side. "Load of nosey parkers!"

He put his fingers to his nose and sprayed them out in a fan. A small boy standing in the street promptly did the same thing back.

"What's the matter with them?" demanded Ben-Muzzy, irritably. "Haven't they ever seen a broomstick before?"

"They are not common in this part of the world," said Gemma. "And in fact," she added, as Joel transferred his fingers to his ears and began to waggle them, "if you carry on like that someone will probably call the police and have you arrested."

"Pooh! Fiddlesticks! How could they arrest me, on a broomstick?"

"They'd come up in their helicopter," said Gemma. "I knew it was asking for trouble, flying through the streets in broad daylight."

"I could understand if it was a pig," said Ben-Muzzy. "I mean, pigs might fly and the moon might be made of green cheese. But a common-or-garden *broomstick* – "

"You see," said Gemma, "people just aren't used to them."

"Well, I can't stand much more of this," declared Ben-Muzzy. They were over the High Street, now, and all the shoppers were lining the pavements, their heads tipped back as they stared up at the broomstick. "I shall have to make us invisible."

"Oh, great stuff!" Gemma bounced excitedly, forgetting that a bouncy broomstick made her sick. She had never been turned invisible before. (Joel had, and had never stopped boasting about it for months on end. "When I was *invisible*..." he'd kept saying.)

Ben-Muzzy took off his hat and tossed it up into the air.

"By the powers of wizardry,
Make it so they cannot see
Neither twins nor stick nor me."

"That wasn't the spell you said last time,"
said Joel. "The time you made me invisible.
The spell you s— " He broke off. "Oops!" he
said. "I'm going!"

Gemma watched in fascination as bit by bit
her twin disappeared. By the time she thought
to look at herself, she, too, had disappeared.
So had the broomstick, though fortunately
she could still feel it beneath her. It was a very
strange sensation, knowing that you were
there yet not being able to see yourself. She
could understand, now, why Joel had kept
talking about it.

They flew on, over the High Street, round
the Town Hall, past the station; one invisible
wizard and two invisible twins on an invisible
broomstick.

"Look!" said Gemma. "There's Mr
Huddle!"

Mr Huddle was the caretaker from school.

"Let's go and buzz him!" urged Joel, but
Gemma thought it wouldn't be kind. It was
true that Mr Huddle had occasionally ticked
them off for throwing conkers through the
open window of the secretary's office or for
climbing on the roof of the infants'
cloakroom, but he was old and frail. It might
frighten him to be buzzed by an invisible
broomstick.

"Spoilsport!" yelled Joel. There were times
when Gemma simply wasn't any fun at all.

"Where is this *Retsof Maharg* person?"
Ben-Muzzy wanted to know.

"Pardon?" Joel blinked.

"Graham Foster," said Gemma.

"Oh! The nerd. We're nearly there. Turn
left at the next corner and he's halfway down
... I'll know it when we get there. There's a
gnome in the front garden."

"A gnome?" Ben-Muzzy sounded startled.
"You didn't say anything about gnomes!"

"It's all right, it's not a real one," said Joel.
"It's a garden gnome."

"Even so. Gnomes can turn very nasty,"
said Ben-Muzzy.

"Not garden gnomes. They're kind of like ... *tame* gnomes." Joel flung out an arm, nearly knocking Gemma off the broomstick. "There it is, over there!"

The garden gnome sat all by itself on a spotted mushroom in the middle of the grass. It wore a red pointed hat and was puffing on a pipe.

"That's a *gnome*?" said Ben-Muzzy. "Not like any gnome I've ever seen!"

He circled twice, nonetheless, just to satisfy himself that it was not going to do anything, then took the broomstick skimming over the roof to land neatly in the back garden, behind a flowering shrub.

"You're getting ever so much better," said Gemma. "Before when you landed it always used to make my stomach go blurp."

"I'm getting better at everything," boasted Ben-Muzzy. "My spells hardly ever go wrong now. Wollibar even let me have a stir of the cauldron the other day."

"Wow!" said Gemma.

Joel was growing impatient. He wanted to get on with frightening Graham Foster.

"Come on!" he said. "Turn us into witches!"

"All three of us?" said Ben-Muzzy.

"Oh, I suppose she can be one if she wants."

Gemma wasn't sure that she did. "I don't think it's very nice to frighten people."

"Shall I tell you something?" said Joel. He thrust an invisible face towards her. She could feel his breath as he spoke. "You are becoming one big *pain*!"

"So are you," said Gemma, pushing at him. "You're becoming a yob. Go and play your silly little tricks; I'll stay here and look after the broomstick. You might as well leave me invisible," she told Ben Muzzy. "I wouldn't want anyone to think I was mixed up in it."

"Girls!" said Joel.

"Boys!" said Gemma.

She stuck out her tongue, and probably Joel did, too, though she couldn't actually see it. But it was what he usually did.

"I'm casting the spell now," warned Ben-Muzzy. "Watch out for the hat!"

Gemma felt something brush past her nose. Then she heard Ben-Muzzy, chanting:

"At the count of number three,
Turn to witches,
Joel and me!"

Gemma counted, inside herself, "One –
two – three – "

As she reached number three, she had to
put a hand to her mouth to stifle a scream:
there in front of her stood two withered-
looking hags, red of eye and sharp of fang,
wearing tall steeple hats and flapping black
cloaks like ravens' wings. She couldn't even
tell which was Ben-Muzzy and which was
Joel.

"Now for it!" cackled one, rubbing his
clawlike hands with their long, horny
fingernails. Maybe that was Joel.

"I still think you're being mean," said Gemma. Graham Foster might be a nerd, but he probably couldn't help it and it wasn't his fault he had broken the glass. And goodness knows, the witches were enough to frighten Gemma, and Gemma *knew* that they were only her twin and Ben-Muzzy.

"Why don't we just go for a nice ride on the broomstick?" she said.

" 'Cause I don't want to go for a nice ride!" cackled the witch that was probably Joel. "I want to go and play tricks on Graham Foster!"

"We could visit Wonderland and go up the Dream Ladder."

"Wonderland's for girls," sneered the witch. Definitely Joel. Gemma sighed.

"Well, don't be long. I'll get bored just standing here."

"That's your problem," said the witch.

The two of them went flapping and croaking up the garden, leaving Gemma to stand guard over the invisible broomstick. She could hear them sniggering, in a witchlike way, as they laid their plans. She was surprised at Ben-Muzzy; she hadn't thought he was quite as silly as her twin.

"What we'll do," Joel was croaking as they drew near the house, "we'll peep in at the window and see if we can see him, and if we can – "

"We'll jump up and down – "

"And pull hideous faces – "

"And go *aieeeeeeeeeeeee*!"

"That's what we'll do," agreed Joel. It would pay Graham Foster back for getting Joel into trouble. Mr Batty had been really mad at Joel about that broken glass. (It just so happened that Joel had broken three the week before when he and Simon Bone had been having a food-flicking contest.)

The two witches crept up to the window and peered in. What luck! There was Graham Foster, all by himself, in front of the television.

The witches jumped up and down, flapping their cloaks. Graham Foster sat, glued to the television set. *Flap!* went the witches. *Zip, zap* went Graham Foster's eyes, following the action on the screen.

The witches redoubled their efforts, hooting and screeching and thrashing about in the flower-bed. At last Graham Foster looked up. His eyes, as he saw the witches, went round as satellite dishes. His cheeks grew pale as fungus.

The witches curled back their lips over their pointed teeth and rolled their eyeballs in their sockets and flared the nostrils of their long thin noses.

"*Aieeeeeeeeeeeee!*" they howled.

Graham Foster leapt out of his chair and ran from the room in terror.

"Hoo hoo hoo!" sniggered the witches. They were having the time of their lives.

Suddenly, from the side of the house, came a woman's voice. "What's the matter, Graham? What do you mean, witches? You've been watching too much television. Go on, Rover! Out you go. Be a good boy!"

The next minute, an enormous woolly dog had come bounding into the garden. It took one look at the witches and pounced: the witches took one look at the dog and ran.

"Wah!" cried Joel.

"Help!" cried Ben-Muzzy.

"Get the broomstick!" they screamed, together.

Pathetic, thought Gemma. It was only a dog; it only wanted to play. She dragged the invisible broomstick out into the open.

"Quick!" panted Joel.

"Hurry!" puffed Ben-Muzzy.

"Where is it?" they wailed.

"Right here," said Gemma. "In front of you."

"Where?"

"I can't see it!"

"I can't – *ow*!"

The big woolly dog, in playful mood, had lunged forward and seized part of a witch's cloak between its teeth.

"Grr-uff!" went the dog, shaking the cloak to and fro.

There was a scream from the witch (Joel or Ben-Muzzy?) and the sound of ripping material. From the house came the woman's voice. "Rover! What have you got out there?"

The two witches began to panic and flap about in circles.

"Quick!"

"Help!"

"Do something!"

Gemma shook her head. Firmly, she took a

witch's hand in each of hers and placed them on the broomstick. They still went on flapping and panicking.

"Where is it?"

"I can't feel it!"

"Help!"

"Quick!"

"Do something!"

"I am doing something," said Gemma, crossly. "Get on the broomstick and take us out of this garden before the police come and arrest you!"

"*Ereh morf,*" babbled Ben-Muzzy, "*ereh morf yawa su ekat!*"

The invisible broomstick, with its crew of two witches and one invisible twin, rose into the air just in time. Another second and the big woolly dog would have run straight into them.

"Phew!" breathed Joel. "That was a close one!"

"Serves you right," said Gemma. "Playing around being witches... You look ridiculous!"

Joel never liked to be told that he looked ridiculous.

"Let's land somewhere, quick, and change ourselves back," he said anxiously.

"L-land where?" Ben Muzzy was still shaking. It made the broomstick tremble right along its length.

"Land anywhere," said Gemma, "before I get sick!"

"Erehw-wyna d-dnal," stammered Ben-Muzzy.

The broomstick promptly headed for the nearest building, which happened to be the police station.

"No!" shrieked Joel.

"On?" said Ben-Muzzy.

"No!" said Joel.

"On," said Ben-Muzzy.

"Why do you keep shouting on when I'm telling you no?" screamed Joel.

"N— "

"Don't!" howled Gemma, as the broomstick, by now thoroughly confused, circled the police station, preparing to land. (A little knot of policemen was already standing outside, exclaiming at the sight of two flying witches.) Didn't Joel understand broomstick talk even yet? The last thing they wanted Ben-Muzzy to say was *no*. No in broomstick talk meant on. *On* in broomstick talk meant no.

"Tell it *on*," said Gemma, sternly.

"*O-on,*" stammered Ben-Muzzy.

To Gemma's relief, the broomstick righted itself and soared upwards, out of sight.

"You really do need your heads examined," grumbled Gemma. "You'd better get it to take us somewhere private."

The witch that was Ben-Muzzy wiped a trembling claw across its brow. "*Etavirp – erehwemos – su ekat.*"

"Somewhere *very* private," said Joel. He didn't want anyone catching sight of him in this state.

"*Etavirp – yrev erehwemos.*"

The broomstick made a sudden turn right. Where was it going now? wondered Gemma. They were flying along a river; could it be the Thames?

"Look!" Joel pointed. "The Houses of Parliament!"

"We don't want to go there!"

They weren't going to the Houses of Parliament. The broomstick had been told to take them somewhere private, and somewhere private was where it was taking them. The most private place in the whole of London...

Chapter Three

Whoosh! went the broomstick, zipping through an open window.

They were in the most private place in the whole of London. It seemed to be somebody's bedroom. A woman was seated at a dressing table, trying on a tiara. It was the Queen! They were in the Queen's bedroom!

Gemma screamed. The Queen swung round and bumped into the invisible broomstick. The Queen screamed. Then she saw the two horrible hags and screamed even louder. Immediately, the door flew open and two guards came bursting in.

"Quick!" yelled Joel. "Get us out of here!"

"Tuo!" cried Gemma.

"Tuo," bleated Ben-Muzzy.

The broomstick zipped back through the window just in time; another second and the guards would have been on them.

"Wow!" said Joel. "That could have been nasty."

"Where was it?" whispered Ben-Muzzy.

"It was Buckingham Palace," said Gemma. "We could have ended up in *prison*. You – " she poked at Joel – "you and your somewhere very private!"

"Well, you think of somewhere, then," sulked Joel.

"Tell it to land in the park, behind the trees. No one'll see us there. *Krap eht ni dnal*," said Gemma. She was beginning to get the hang of broomstick talk. *Krap eht ni dnal*: land in the park.

"Which park?" said Joel.

"Any park!"

"We can't go to *any* park. You've got to say *which* park."

"Witch park?" In his haste to take them somewhere, Ben-Muzzy snatched eagerly at a familiar word. *"Krap hctiw eht ni dnal,"* gabbled Ben-Muzzy.

The broomstick obediently upended itself and shot headfirst into the sunset. Wherever it was going, it was going there very fast.

"Hctiw," thought Gemma, rolling the word about her head. *"Huh-kuh-ti-w." Huh-kuh-ti-w?* She tried it the other way round. *"W-it-kuh-huh – "*

The broomstick had slid into a long downward curve. It was racing, now, like a horse heading for home. From somewhere below came sounds which made Gemma's blood freeze in her veins. Dreadful curses and cacklings and screeches of laughter.

"On!" screeched Gemma.

"No?" said Ben-Muzzy.

"No! I mean – *no*! I mean ... ON!"

"Oh, don't start that again," complained Joel. "For goodness' – aaaaargh!" yelled Joel, suddenly catching sight of what was lying in

wait for them: dozens of pairs of blood-red eyes, gleaming through the darkness.

"Witches!" moaned Joel.

"ON!" roared Gemma and Ben-Muzzy, with all the force they were capable of.

"Fast!" added Gemma. *"Tsaf, tsaf, tsaf!"*

The broomstick moved, *tsaf*. You could tell it was reluctant, but fortunately it had been well trained.

"Now what do we do?" demanded Joel.

Gemma leaned forward. She reached past Joel and tapped Ben-Muzzy on the shoulder.

"Say after me ... *seert – eht – dniheb –* "

"S-seert – eht – d-dniheb – "

"Krap – ruo – ni – dnal."

"Krap – r-ruo – ni – d-dnal."

"Right." *Land in our park,* Gemma thought. Gemma sat back. She wondered if there would be headlines in tomorrow's papers.

INTRUDERS IN QUEEN'S BEDROOM: QUEEN SEES

WITCHES. Left to themselves, she thought, Joel and Ben-Muzzy really were quite useless. They would be lost without Gemma.

The broomstick landed in the park, behind the trees, exactly where Gemma had told it to. (*Blurp*, went Gemma's stomach, as Ben-Muzzy lost control.)

The two witches stepped off. One of them trod on its cloak and fell over. Gemma giggled. She wasn't scared of them any more; they looked too silly.

"Change me back!" commanded Joel. "Quick, before I get stuck like it!"

"All right, all r-right! I c-can't do every-th-thing at once," said Ben-Muzzy, whose teeth were still chattering at the narrowness of their escape from the witches' park. "And anyw-way I'll n-need your help... I haven't g-got my w-wizard's hat."

"So how did you manage just now?" said Gemma. "When you were being a witch all by yourself?"

"Ah, that was very clever," said Ben-Muzzy. "I did a spell that self-destructed."

"That sounds advanced," said Gemma.

"Yes, it is, but I only know how to do it for one person."

"Look, can we just get on with things?" said Joel. He didn't want to stay as a witch for the rest of his life. "I can see some oak trees over there."

The twins knew enough about magic by now to know that if you didn't have a black cat (or a wizard's hat) then you had to have three oak trees and form a circle inside them. Joel flapped his way towards them, followed by Ben-Muzzy and the still invisible Gemma carrying the still invisible broomstick.

Gemma hoped Ben-Muzzy didn't run out of magic before he made her visible again. Once he'd run out it could take ages before it came back.

"Right." Ben-Muzzy became businesslike. "Form a circle." He held out his hands. The twins took hold of them. "Three steps to the right, three steps to the left...

"We no longer wish to be
Witches made by wizardry.
Turn us back to what we were,
A twin called Joel and wizard fair."

"Wizard *fair*?" said Gemma, as her twin and Ben-Muzzy materialized before her.

"You see, it has to rhyme." Ben-Muzzy said it apologetically. "I know it's not very good poetry, but it was all I could think of. You ought to hear Wollibar... *'To spell or not to spell, that is the question...'*, *'Shall I compare thee to a summer's spell...'*, *'Friends, wizards, countrymen, spell me your ears –* ' "

"Mm. Well," said Gemma, "so long as it does the trick I suppose that's all that matters."

"It hasn't done the trick!" Joel suddenly let out a loud howl. "I thought it was supposed

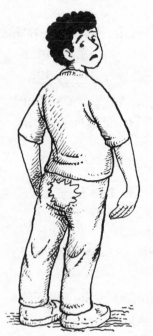

to put me back the way I was. Look at me!"

They looked. There was a large chunk missing from the seat of Joel's jeans. Gemma chortled, happily.

"I can see your knickers! They're bright yellow!"

Joel's face grew tomato-coloured. "You'd jolly well better do something,"

-46-

he said to Ben-Muzzy. "My mum'll go mad if she sees this. These are new jeans, these are."

"It shouldn't have happened," said Ben-Muzzy, worried. "I don't know how it got through."

"It was the dog," said Gemma.

"Yes, but when I said take us *back*, we should have turned *back*. You shouldn't be *able* to see his knickers."

"Well, I can," said Gemma. "Bright yellow!"

"You'd just jolly well better do something," said Joel.

Resigned, Ben-Muzzy took off his hat and lobbed it into the air. Droningly, he recited:

"Fill the gap, mend the jeans,
Make them whole by any means.
Also Gemma and the stick
Would like to be less clear, more thick."

It was a relief to be visible again, thought Gemma, carefully examining herself, but Ben-Muzzy really ought to try a bit harder with his poetry. Anyone could make up a silly little jingle like that. Perhaps she should lend him her rhyming dictionary.

She looked up to find Joel doubtfully fingering his backside.

"What's happened?" he said.

"You've now got a bright yellow patch," Gemma informed him. "But it's all right, I can't see your knickers any more."

"A patch?" said Joel. "A *patch*? On my new jeans?"

"It's the best I can do. I'm not *made* of magic," said Ben-Muzzy. He said it rather testily. Just because he was a wizard, some people seemed to think he had an unlimited supply. "I want to keep what I've got left for playing a trick on this witch."

Joel wondered whether to make an angry scene or whether to live with his patch. In the end, he decided he might as well live with his patch. After all, it was quite trendy, and he was looking forward to playing a trick on some grungy old witch.

"So what exactly are we going to do?" he said.

Ben-Muzzy's eyes gleamed. "I thought what we'd do, we'd turn ourselves into black cats and fly over the cave, spitting!"

"Hey, brilliant!" cried Joel. "When do we get to turn into them?"

"Do it now, if you like."

"No, *thank* you," said Gemma.

"He didn't mean you," said Joel. "You can just sit at the back and keep quiet."

Gemma humped her shoulders, rather huffily. She had never heard anything so pathetic! Turning themselves into black cats just to make fun of some poor silly old witch.

"Anyway," said Gemma, "what about your magic? You don't want to use it all up."

"I shall use what I need to use." Ben-Muzzy said it with cold dignity. "This is the purpose of our mission."

"What, frightening a silly old witch?"

"He's been dared!" said Joel.

"So what?"

Joel stared at her, shocked. "So he's got to do it!"

"Why?"

"Well, because – because he has! His honour's at stake." Of course, you couldn't expect a girl to understand. "Come on! Let's get turned into cats!"

Gemma, rather scornfully, bent down to examine the bristles on the broomstick. (Lovely and clean! They were obviously brushed every day.) She heard Ben-Muzzy's voice, chanting some more of his bad poetry:

"Joel and Ben-Muzzy, we
Two black cats would like to be."

Well, at least black cats were better to look at than witches – and at least you could tell them apart. The black cat that was Joel had a small clump of yellow fur on his backside.

"All right, so where are we going?" said Gemma, as they remounted the broomstick.

"To find the grungy old witch!" cried the cat that was Joel.

"Evac eht ot su ekat! Hctiw eht fo evac eht!"

The broomstick rose carefully into the air

and swung out in a wide arc across the town. Fortunately by now it was dusk and there were not so many people about. One or two glanced up and thought just for a moment that they could see two black cats and a twin riding on a broomstick, but of course that wasn't possible. They rubbed their eyes and looked again and the broomstick had gone.

"How shall we know when we've got there?" said Gemma.

"We shall know," said Ben-Muzzy.

Over land, over sea, over the tops of shining mountains, over rivers and lakes and oceans, across deserts, across plains, round great tall cities and barren rocky hillsides, through sunshine and snow, the broomstick flew on.

"When you've done this stupid thing," said Gemma, "this stupid thing that you've been dared, can we go to Wonderland?"

"No," said Joel, at the same time as Ben-Muzzy called, "Hold tight! Something's happened!"

The black cats dug their claws in. Gemma clung fast with both hands. The broomstick was suddenly behaving most erratically, weaving and twisting and turning in circles.

"Are we there?" asked Gemma.

"Yes, but something seems to be blocking us... *Gniog peek!*" instructed Ben-Muzzy. "*Drawrof!*"

The broomstick, obviously not happy, edged nervously forward. It stopped, with a shudder.

"*Drawrof!*" roared Ben-Muzzy.

The broomstick quivered. It plainly didn't want to go.

"*Yas I sa od!*" bellowed Ben-Muzzy, swishing his long black cat's tail.

Gemma could almost hear the broomstick heave a sigh. Obediently it launched itself full steam ahead. The next second, it was rocketing backwards, out of control, twisting, turning, looping the loop.

The broomstick landed nose down, like a dart, sticking in the earth. On legs that were far from steady, Gemma slid off.

"W-what happened?"

The cat that was Ben-Muzzy hissed, angrily. "She's gone and put a force field round herself! She must have done it after Podnock's visit."

You couldn't really blame her, thought Gemma. Who wanted a gang of jeering wizards flying over their backyard?

"Well, that's that, then," she said. "That's knocked that idea on the head. *Now* can we go to Wonderland?"

"No, we can't! I told you," said the black cat, irritably, "I've been *dared*. If I can't get there one way, I'll get there another!"

"Dunno how," said Gemma. She sat down on the grass, next to the broomstick. They had landed on the top of a hill, with countryside stretching in all directions as far as the eye could see.

"This is nice," said Gemma. She yawned and lay back. "I've had enough excitement for the moment. You two do whatever you want... Go and catch some mice or something. Behave like *real* cats."

When Gemma opened her eyes a few minutes later, the black cats had disappeared and in their place were Joel in his patched jeans and Ben-Muzzy in his green cloak and wizard's hat. They had their heads together. She heard Joel say, "Could just leave her here."

Gemma sprang into a sitting position. "You're not leaving me anywhere!"

"Oh. It's awake," said Joel, disappointed.

"Yes, I am! What are you plotting?"

"We're working out how to find the grungy witch. She can't be too far away."

"There's a signpost over there." Ben-Muzzy pointed, flapping his cloak. "Let's go and see what it says."

Gemma scrambled to her feet, Ben-Muzzy picked up the broomstick and they set off down the hillside.

"Well, it doesn't say Grungy Old Witch," said Gemma. What it said, pointing back up the hill, was PROVERBIAL VILLAGE. Gemma

studied it a while, puzzled. "How can you have a village called Proverbial?"

"Why shouldn't you have a village called Proverbial?" Joel always liked to argue with Gemma. "It's obviously its name. Like London or Manchester or Kingston-on-Thames."

It didn't seem much like London or Manchester to Gemma. *Or* like Kingston-on-Thames. You couldn't have a village called Proverbial!

Joel and Ben-Muzzy, who never bothered their heads about such matters, were already walking on. Gemma skipped after them, still puzzled.

"It seems very odd to me," puffed Gemma,

as they toiled back up the side of the hill.

"Yes, well, it would to you," said Joel. "Not to normal people."

They crawled up the hill until they reached the top, only to find that they immediately had to start going down again.

"How utterly ridiculous," grumbled Gemma, who had given herself a stitch.

"What goes up must come down," said Joel.

Stupid know-all!

They stood for a moment on the ridge of the hill, gazing out at a winding road and a distant cluster of houses. Below them, a man in a brown track suit was rolling an enormous boulder down the hillside.

"If he'd been coming up," said Ben-Muzzy, "we could have asked him if he knew the way to the witch."

"He is coming up," said Gemma. "Look!"

They watched, curiously, as the man staggered back to the top, carrying his boulder in his arms. Before they could call out to him, he had set the boulder down, given it a push and started off all over again.

"Interesting," said Joel.

"Very," said Gemma.

Ben-Muzzy wondered what was interesting about a man rolling a boulder down a hill. It seemed a bit pointless, if you asked him.

"Let's go and find out what he's doing it for!"

Already Gemma was capering off, closely followed by Joel and rather more slowly by Ben-Muzzy.

"Excuse me!" said Gemma.

"Not at all," said the man, politely.

He continued on his way down the hill, the

twins hopping after him.

"What are you doing?" said Gemma.

"I should have thought," said the man, giving her a strange look, "that it was perfectly obvious what I was doing... I'm rolling this stone down this hill."

"Yes, I can see that," said Gemma. "We just wondered why you were doing it."

The man stopped, carefully inspected his boulder, hoisted it back into his arms and went stumbling off again to the top of the hill. The twins, stitches quite forgotten, danced at his side. (Ben-Muzzy sat down under a tree to wait. The twins were very easily sidetracked; he had noticed it before.)

"Why *are* you doing it?" said Gemma.

"What a very ignorant little girl you must be." The man looked at her, sternly, over the top of his boulder. "Don't you know your proverbs? 'A rolling stone gathers no moss'?"

"Of course I know that!" Gemma said it indignantly. She resented being called ignorant.

"Well, there you are, then." The man set down the boulder, gave it a push with the toe of his shoe and off they went all over again, following the boulder down the hill. "I'm proving it. I'm *proving* that a rolling stone gathers no moss."

"What for?" said Joel, feeling that it was about time he made his mark on the conversation. "Everyone already knows it!"

"No, they do not. How could they? It hasn't been proved yet. It's a lifetime's work, proving proverbs. Why, I've been rolling this stone down this hill for more years than I can remember, and my father and grandfather before me. We've rolled this stone," said the man, "down every hillside in the land."

"And when will you definitely be able to say that it's gathered no moss?" Joel asked the question, solemnly.

"Ah! That'll be for the proverbs committee to decide. That's not up to me. I just get on with my job as best I can."

The twins thought about this a while.

"What would happen if one day someone proved a proverb was wrong?" said Joel.

The man scratched his head.

"No one would prove a stupid thing like that," he said. "There wouldn't be any point in it, would there?"

He hoisted the boulder into his arms and turned back up the hill.

"Now you know," said Joel, "why it's called Proverbial Village."

"Brilliant!" said Gemma. "Let's walk on. We might find more of them!"

"More of what?" said Ben-Muzzy, scrambling up from beneath his tree.

"People proving proverbs."

"We didn't come here to find people proving proverbs, we came to find a witch! Did you ask him?"

"Oh, no!" Joel clapped a hand to his mouth. "I forgot!"

"Don't worry about the soppy old witch," said Gemma. "This is much more fun!"

"But it's not why we came," said Joel.

"No, it's not!" Ben-Muzzy was growing agitated. He couldn't go back to Podnock and admit that he had failed. Podnock would never let him live it down.

"It's all right," said Joel. "We'll ask the next person that we see."

Chapter Four

The next person they saw was a man having a picnic. It was a very strange sort of picnic. There wasn't any food, just hundreds of cans of drink: orange squash, ginger beer, Coca Cola, a carton of milk, a bottle of mineral water, a pot of tea, a pot of coffee, lemon barley, Cherry Fizz, vegetable soup, even gravy browning.

The twins, nudging each other, stopped to watch. Ben-Muzzy sighed. He didn't see anything particularly interesting in people proving proverbs. It might amuse the twins, but to a wizard it seemed rather infantile.

As the twins stood watching, the man solemnly poured out a glass of gravy browning. He raised it to his lips, but before he could drink it his hand had shaken and the gravy browning had spilled all over the bib he had tied under his chin. The bib was already stained with orange squash and coffee.

The man picked up a carton of milk and poured some out. Halfway to his mouth the milk went splashing over the side to join the gravy browning and the orange squash and the coffee on his bib.

"There must be something wrong with him," whispered Gemma. "He must have some kind of shaking disease."

The man, unfortunately, heard her. He looked up and glared.

"Just watch your manners, child!"

"I do beg your pardon," said Gemma. An

idea struck her. "Are you proving something?"

"There's many a slip 'twixt cup and lip!" shouted Joel, triumphantly.

"Well, of course there is!" snapped the man. "You don't think I'm spilling things over myself just for the fun of it, do you?"

The twins exchanged glances and shook with silent giggles. They ran up the road and leaned against a fence and laughed until the tears rolled down their cheeks. Ben-Muzzy slowly shook his head. Perhaps, he thought sadly, wizards didn't have any sense of humour. He wondered whether to ask the drinking man about the witch, but by now the drinking man was in such a rage that he was simply picking up glasses and hurling the contents down his bib as fast as he could.

"Shaking disease!" he was muttering. "Shaking disease!"

Ben-Muzzy hurried off after the twins. He didn't fancy having a cup of coffee or a bowl of soup thrown over his clean cloak.

Very soon they came to a row of houses, and then a parade of shops. Among the shops was a building which said BANK in large gold letters. As they walked past it a man ran out and stared furtively up and down the street. He was wearing a mask and a long stripy jersey and carrying a sack labelled SWAG. From the bank came a shout of "Stop, thief!"

The man darted up a side road. Joel immediately darted after him. Gemma and Ben-Muzzy, after a moment's rather startled hesitation, dashed off in pursuit. No one else in the street took the slightest bit of notice. People weren't at all public spirited, thought Gemma, as she pounded after Joel and the thief.

The thief vaulted over a wall and into someone's back garden. Joel vaulted after him. Together, first the thief and then Joel, they trampled over a flower-bed, squeezed through a gap in the fence, and raced up an alleyway. Joel was having a splendid time! All his life he had dreamed of something like this happening. He wondered if he would have his picture taken and be interviewed for television.

The thief dropped his swag bag and stooped to pick it up. Joel was on him in a flash. By the time Gemma and Ben-Muzzy arrived the thief was flat on his back with Joel sitting on his chest and pummelling him.

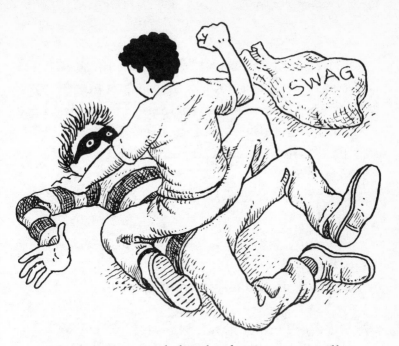

"Stop it!" roared the thief. "Stop it, I tell you!"

"Not likely!" said Joel. He glanced round, impatiently, at his twin and Ben-Muzzy. "Well, don't just stand there gawping! Go and find a policeman!"

"Oh, all right," said Gemma; but before she could move they heard the sound of running footsteps and another man appeared. He, too, was wearing a long stripy jersey. At the sight of Joel sitting on the thief, he screeched to a halt.

"What are you doing?" he asked, turning very pale.

"I've caught a thief!" Joel announced it, proudly. "Are you a plainclothes copper?"

"No, I'm not," said the man. He stamped a foot. "I'm a thief and I was set to catch a thief. Now you've gone and ruined everything!"

"Get off my chest," ordered the first thief, angrily.

"I think they must have been proving proverbs," hissed Gemma.

Slowly, Joel removed himself from the thief's chest.

"I don't understand," he said.

"Well, you ought," said the second thief. "Really, whatever am I going to do?"

"It's his first day on the job," said thief number one, picking up his swag bag and brushing the dust off it. "You might have shown a little more consideration. A joke's a joke, but this has gone too far. I didn't mind you chasing me, but you might have let him do the catching."

"Well, how was I to know he was after you?" said Joel.

"You should have known!" The second thief burst into tears. "Set a thief to catch a thief. Everyone knows that. I've spent six months training to work on proverbs and now you have to come along and spoil it on my very first day. It's so unfair!"

"I'm sorry," said Joel, "but I've never heard of that proverb. I didn't know you had to have thieves to catch other thieves. I thought anyone could do it."

"They're not supposed to," sniffed the man. "Now you've made me lose confidence. I shall never be the same again."

The two thieves linked arms and went walking off together. It didn't seem quite the right moment to ask about the grungy witch.

"This is what I call a really dumb kind of place," said Ben-Muzzy.

"Do you think so?" said Gemma. "I think it's brilliant!"

Gemma could have stayed here for ever. She thought of other proverbs that she knew. People in glass houses shouldn't throw stones (that would be a good one!); A stitch in time saves nine; More haste, less—

"What's that?" Ben-Muzzy had stopped and was twitching his nostrils. "Something's burning!"

Clouds of smoke were billowing from an open window. At any other time the twins

would have rushed to call the fire brigade,
but in Proverbial Village they were learning
to be more cautious.

"Alfred and the Cakes?" said Joel.

Gemma looked at him, scornfully. "That's
not a proverb! That's history."

"Well, I know *that*," said Joel, who in fact,
just for a moment, had got a bit muddled.

They peered in, through the window.

"Blimey!" said Joel.

Through the thick blanket of smoke could
be seen a crowd of men in white aprons and
tall chef's hats, all squabbling over a stove.
Several of them seemed to be trying to stir
something in the same saucepan.

"Too many cooks spoil the broth!"
whispered Gemma. "I wonder what they're

supposed to be cooking?"

Who cares? thought Ben-Muzzy. Glumly, he
propped himself against the wall. A fine All
Spells' Night this was turning out to be!

Inside the kitchen, the battle raged fast and
furious.

One of the chefs picked up a bag of flour
and threw the contents at the stove. Another
chef promptly picked up a wooden spoon and
hit him on the head.

"Leave off!" he shouted. "We don't want
flour in the vegetables!"

Another of the chefs was doing his best to
empty a pepper pot into the saucepan.
Another was standing at a distance and
lobbing potatoes across the kitchen. Two
more were fighting each other with rolling

pins. Some kept turning the gas up, some kept turning it down, and all the time thick plumes of smoke were rolling out of the window.

"Oh, stop it!" cried the man with the wooden spoon, as the man with the bag of flour seized a handful of currants and tossed them into the pan. "You're ruining my vegetables!"

"I hope you haven't put too much salt in that pan," said the other man, dangerously. "I told you I was baking a cake."

"You don't bake cakes in saucepans," said Gemma, loudly.

The two men stopped quarrelling and turned to stare at her.

"There you are," said the man who was cooking vegetables. "You don't bake cakes in saucepans."

He turned victoriously away and began hitting everyone in sight with the wooden spoon.

"Turn the gas up, turn the gas up, the vegetables aren't boiling!"

The man who was baking a cake came over to the window.

"Hallo," he said. "Would you like to taste something?"

"Yes, please!" said Joel, who never refused an offer of food.

"Good!" said the man. "I've got just the thing for you. Wait there."

He returned through the clouds of smoke and fought his way across to a table.

"There!" he said, coming back to the window. "Try a spoonful of this and tell me what you think."

He set a large blue pot on the window ledge and removed the lid. Joel recoiled. So did Gemma.

"What is it?" said Joel.

"Broth! Beautiful broth! Freshly made this morning. Try some!"

Dubiously, Joel took the spoon that was being held out to him. If he hadn't known that it was broth he would have said it was dirty washing-up water full of all the old scrapings off people's plates.

"Go on, then!" said Gemma, glad it hadn't been offered to her. "Taste it!"

Bravely, Joel stuck the spoon into his mouth and swallowed. A shudder ran through him. It was worse than dirty washing-up water. It was even worse than school dinners. It was like stale-feet-cheese and something off the compost heap.

"Well?" said the cook, anxiously. "What do you think?"

After his experience with the thief, Joel knew that he had to be careful. He didn't want to upset any more people.

"Yeah, it was – it was all right," he said. "Some of the best broth I've ever tasted."

"*What?*" The cook turned purple. He choked, and slammed the pot back on to the table. "This child," he announced, "says that our broth is the best broth he's ever tasted!"

A shocked silence fell over the kitchen. All the other cooks stopped hitting one another with rolling pins and wooden spoons. They gathered round the window and stared in disbelief at Joel.

"But – but it can't be!" protested the man who had thrown potatoes. "He must be having us on!"

"It can't be our fault," said another. "We've always managed to spoil the broth before."

"There are too many of you," explained Gemma. "You're bound to spoil it if you're all doing different things at the same time in the same saucepan."

"Exactly!" said the first man. "That's why I

can't understand it."

It slowly occurred to Joel that he had made yet another mistake. He should have told the truth and said the broth was too horrible to eat, then everyone would have been happy.

"Try giving some to him," said Gemma, pointing at Ben-Muzzy. "See what he thinks of it."

The cook leaned out of the window.

"Hi, you!" he said.

"Me?" said Ben-Muzzy.

"Yes! Would you care for some broth?"

"Thank you," said Ben-Muzzy, absently. He took the spoon and put it into his mouth. Everyone waited.

"Yeeeeeeeeeurgh!" howled Ben-Muzzy.

"That was disgusting!"

From inside the kitchen, a great cheer went up.

"Disgusting! He said it was disgusting!"

"Turn the gas down, turn the gas down! The vegetables are boiling over!"

All the cooks surged back to the stove. In another moment they were happily squabbling again and the smell of burning was worse than ever.

"Phew!" said Joel. "I thought they were going to start whacking me!"

"That's twice you've upset people." Gemma said it reproachfully. "You're just not safe to be with."

"All the more reason for getting out of here," urged Ben-Muzzy.

"Yeah! We're supposed to be looking for the grungy old witch!" Joel set off down the street at a caper. "We'll ask the first person we see!"

"I'll ask," said Gemma. "Not you."

It wasn't easy, finding someone to ask. All the people in Proverbial Village seemed so busy proving proverbs that she scarcely liked to interrupt any of them.

They saw a woman emptying a pail of

soapsuds out of a window ("Washing her dirty linen in public!" giggled Gemma), a man in a glasshouse throwing stones at another man in a glasshouse (with predictable results), a man trying to make bricks out of straw, a woman putting all her eggs into one basket, another woman counting her chickens before they'd hatched, a little party of people attempting to cross their bridges before they came to them – the twins were becoming quite quick at guessing proverbs.

They had walked right through the village from one end to the other before they found anyone who had time to talk. A man wearing T-shirt and shorts waved to them, cheerfully.

"It's a long road that has no turning!"

"I'm sure it must be," agreed Gemma, politely.

"Oh, it is, I can tell you! And this one certainly hasn't any," the man chuckled. "I should know! I've been walking it, come fair weather or foul, these past six years or more. I set off at dawn and I arrive at midnight, then I walk all the way back again."

"Really?" said Gemma. "How interesting! I

don't expect you've ever come across a grungy old witch?"

"Grungy old witch that lives in a cave," said Joel.

"In the middle of a wood," said Ben-Muzzy.

"Ah! You be wanting the wood. Well, now, I have heard tell there's one hereabouts, though I can't say as I've ever seen it myself. You can't, you know, for the trees."

"You can't see the wood for the trees." Gemma nodded.

"That's right! I know the person that's working on it. He's been looking for that wood nigh on thirty years and never come across hide nor hair."

"Just loads and loads of trees."

"Oh! Trees all right. Trees by the score."

"The trees would probably do just as well," said Gemma.

"The trees would do *very* well," said Ben-Muzzy.

"Is that a fact?" The man scratched his head, wonderingly. "Those be they, just over there. If that's what you want."

Gemma looked at Ben-Muzzy. Ben-Muzzy nodded.

"Thank you so much," said Gemma.

"Not at all, a pleasure, I'm sure. You might meet a friend of mine if you're going that way. Give him my regards if you see him. You'll easily recognize him, he's running around with a chicken under his arm."

"A bird in the hand is worth two in the bush?" suggested Joel, before Gemma had time to think of it.

"Stands to reason, really, doesn't it?" agreed the man. "Well, I must bid you good day, I've a long road ahead of me."

"Hope we haven't," said Joel, bounding off towards the wood (which could be seen quite easily in spite of all the trees). "I want to find the grungy witch and start having fun!"

Chapter Five

They bumped into the man with the chicken almost immediately. The chicken was under his arm, squawking.

"It's worth two in the bush," panted the man, as he ran distractedly into a clump of holly.

There was the sound of rustling and trampling, then a loud scream and the man emerged backwards, the chicken clucking indignantly and puffing out its feathers in protest.

"Ow! That hurt!" said the man.

"Well, it would," said Gemma. "Holly's prickly."

"I didn't mean the holly, I meant the chicken... It pecked me! It keeps pecking me! I'm bruised black and blue. It really isn't good enough! They should have given me a canary."

"A chicken is rather large," agreed Gemma, sympathetically. "Even if you managed to find any birds in the bush you wouldn't be able to catch them; not with a chicken under your arm."

"That is not the point. I'm not *supposed* to catch them. I'm supposed to chase them and it's wearing me out!"

"Hey, you don't happen to know a grungy old witch, do you?" cried Joel, before the man could go charging off again.

The man stood poised, ready for flight. "One that lives in a cave?"

"That's the one!" At last they might be getting somewhere. "Lives in a cave in a wood."

"Ah, now, there you have me." The man shook his head. "They do say there's a cave somewhere about, but as to the wood... Which wood, exactly, were you referring to?"

"Well – this one," said Joel.

"This one?" The man slowly swivelled in a

circle, staring about him at the trees. "Which one?"

"This one!" yelled Joel.

"The one we are in *now*," said Ben-Muzzy.

"Sorry. Can't help you there." The man took to his heels and went sprinting off again, heading for a thicket of hawthorn. Over his shoulder, as he ran, he called: "Can't see any wood! Too many trees! Obscure the view!"

"Really," said Ben-Muzzy, "these people are *useless*."

"Oh, what does it matter?" cried Gemma. Gemma was enjoying herself. She went dancing on ahead, down the path. "Who wants to find a grungy old witch?"

"We do," said Joel, loudly. "Silly old moo," he added. Girls had *no* sense of adventure.

"We've wasted enough time already," fretted Ben-Muzzy. "If we don't find her soon – "

At that moment, the ground beneath their feet started shaking.

"Watch out! It's an earthquake!"

Joel flung himself flat, both hands over his head. After a second's startled pause, Ben-Muzzy did likewise. Only Gemma remained upright.

A large furry animal was bounding along the path. It looked a bit like a hand-knitted kangaroo – a kangaroo such as Gemma might knit, full of dropped stitches with a big baggy pouch.

"*Oh!*" cried Gemma, delighted. "It's a furry Walloper!"

Gingerly, Joel and Ben-Muzzy raised their heads. Feeling rather foolish, they got to their feet. They had come across furry Wallopers before, when they had gone to Wonderland. They were the only known animal in the universe that had no brain, but perfectly amiable, for all that.

The Walloper was walloping frantically towards them, rolling his eyes to left and to right.

"They is coming!" he panted. "They is coming!"

"Who's coming?" said Gemma.

"The Smellibots!" panted the Walloper.

"What – " began Gemma, but the Walloper had gone, walloping off in a panic along the path.

"I don't like the sound of this." Joel was looking worried. The Smellibots, whatever they were, must be pretty dangerous if a

creature the size of a Walloper was scared of them. "Maybe we sh—"

"Look!"

Gemma flung out a hand.

A shambling horde of small fluffy objects was coming towards them. They had little round faces like pom-poms, with big brown eyes, tiny twitching noses and soft nibbling mouths. They shuffled on padded feet, front paws held up beneath their chins.

"*Oh!*" Gemma was enchanted. "Aren't they *sweet*?"

"Don't get too close," said Ben-Muzzy.

"Keep away! They might bite!"

Joel made a grab at his twin, but too late: she had already stepped forward, hand outstretched ready to stroke.

"They're so sw— "

The word died on Gemma's lips. Her stomach rose up into her mouth. She pulled out her handkerchief and pressed it to her nose. The stink! The stink was atrocious!

"Eeurgh," went Gemma, into her handkerchief.

Hunched up together, the Smellibots shambled past. Their little pom-pom faces were sad and dejected, their eyes cast down in shame. Behind them danced a procession of imps, red and green, and black and orange, thin as wire and scarcely any taller than the tops of Gemma's trainers. All the imps were holding their noses and squealing, "Ugh!" and "Pooh!" and "Go take a bath!"

"Teeny Meanies," said Ben-Muzzy. His

voice was rather muffled as he had smothered his face in his cloak. It sounded more like "Deedi Beedi".

Some of the Teeny Meanies were carrying sharp-pronged sticks with which they prodded the unfortunate Smellibots in the rear. The Smellibots drooped. Gemma couldn't help but notice that they were accompanied by a buzzing horde of flies.

"Poor little things," she said.

"Dey're not bor." Joel had his nostrils firmly pinched together. "Dey *dink*."

"They are a bit smelly," agreed Gemma, cautiously removing her handkerchief and then hastily clamping it back again. "But maybe they can't help it."

"Of course they can help it." Ben-Muzzy fanned the air with his cloak. "They smell," he said sternly, "because they are *dirty*. Because they obviously never *wash*."

"Maybe no one ever told them to. Maybe we should—"

"Doe!" roared Joel. "We goig fide de grundy wid!"

"I beg your pardon?" said Gemma.

Joel unpinched his nostrils. "I said, we're going to find the grungy witch! At least," he added, "we are if she really exists."

"She does!" said Ben-Muzzy. "She's the biggest joke for miles around! Ask anyone!"

"Seems to me," said Joel, "we already have. Seems to me she's not as well known as you make out. Seems to me—"

In a loud voice Gemma said, "If you're going to quarrel, I shall go on without you."

Gemma continued briskly up the path, trying her best to ignore the last lingering traces of Smellibot. Behind her she could hear Joel telling Ben-Muzzy how girls, and sisters in particular, were nothing but one big pain. Resolutely, Gemma walked on. A black cat was strolling towards her. She held out a hand.

"Hello, cat," said Gemma.

The cat stared haughtily at her. "Hello, *girl*."

Gemma blinked. It had talked! The cat had talked! She turned and called back excitedly to the others, "Hey! This cat can talk!" She swung back to the cat.

"Lovely weather for the time of year, don't you think?"

"All right," said the cat, "if you like this kind of thing."

Gemma reached out to tickle the cat behind its ear.

"Stop her, stop her!" gasped Ben-Muzzy. He broke into a run, his cloak flapping behind him, the broomstick over his shoulder. Black cats were not ordinary cats. You had to know how to handle them.

"There's a nice pussy," crooned Gemma.

The cat tossed its head, pettishly.

"Do you mind? I have just spent half an hour grooming myself. I would rather not have to go through the process all over again."

Gemma pulled a face. "Sorry, I'm sure."

"Ask it about the witch," urged Joel.

"No," said Gemma. "You."

Ben-Muzzy gave a howl, but Joel had already opened his mouth.

"I suppose you don't by any chance happen to know a grungy witch hereabouts?" said Joel.

There was a pause.

"Witch?" said the cat, dangerously.

"Yes, a really grungy one that messes up on her spells and lives in a cave."

"I know of no such person. And if I did, you surely do not suppose that I would tell you? And while we are on the subject – " the cat slid its eyes in Ben-Muzzy's direction – "what, may I ask, are you doing with that broomstick?"

"Oh! What? This?" Ben-Muzzy laughed, nervously. "This isn't a broomstick. This is a – a stick. A broom. A broom in the shape of a stick. A stick that looks like a broom. Just a little thing that I magicked," he said, carelessly.

"I see." The cat looked at the broomstick through narrowed green slits. "It had better be."

"Oh, it is! I assure you!" Ben-Muzzy laughed again, rather more nervously than before. "Totally useless to either witch or wizard. Well, so nice to have met you. We really must be on our way. I'll bid you good—"

"Just one moment!" The cat sprang forward. It sniffed all up and down the length of the broomstick. Its tail swished and writhed. "Where did you get this from?"

"N-nowhere," babbled Ben-Muzzy. "I told you, I magicked it, magicked it, just for the f-fun of it."

The cat quite plainly did not believe him. Gemma remembered the day they had stolen the broomstick from a nest of witches, right under the nose of a black cat that had looked very similar to this one. For all she knew, it could have been this one!

"Well, we'll – we'll bid you good day," said Ben-Muzzy. He gestured frantically to the twins: they got the message. A quick hop onto the broomstick and they could be up and away before the cat realized what was happening.

Ben-Muzzy jumped aboard; the twins scrambled after.

"*Yawa* – " began Ben-Muzzy; but he wasn't fast enough.

"I thought as much!" The cat pounced. "Going somewhere, are you? Allow me!" The cat began to speak very rapidly in advanced broomstick talk. *Eb ot tnaw yeht erehw sloof eseht ekat dna tnavres shctiw a raeh, hctiw a ot degnoleb taht, uoht o!* *

The broomstick shot up into the air.

"Have a nice day, now," purred the cat.

* "O thou, that belonged to a witch, hear a witch's servant and take these fools where they want to be!"

Chapter Six

"Now where are we going?" wailed Gemma. All this toing and froing on a broomstick was not good for her travel sickness.

"I think – " Ben-Muzzy spoke after a long pause – "I think what it said was, Take them where they want to be."

"Oh, well, that's all right, then!" Joel bounced. "What a good thing I asked it!"

Maybe, thought Ben-Muzzy; maybe not. What the cat had actually said was, Take these *fools* where they want to be.

He didn't like the sound of that. It was one thing flying over the witch's cave on a broomstick that you were in control of; quite another being sent there by a black cat. A witch who was capable of putting a force field round herself was capable of anything.

"*Pots!*" said Ben-Muzzy, experimentally; but as he had expected, the broomstick took no notice.

"Why tell it to stop?" yelled Joel. "We're going there, aren't we?"

"I thought," said Gemma, "that it was the whole purpose of your mission?"

Ben-Muzzy made a mumbling sound.

"Because of Podnock," said Gemma, "and his dare. I thought," said Gemma, "that it was a matter of *honour*."

"Podnock only flew over on a broomstick," muttered Ben-Muzzy.

"Well, that's what we seem to be doing, isn't it? Or isn't it?" said Gemma. "No, perhaps it isn't," she said, as the broomstick slowly began to descend. She peered over the side.

"Is this it?" said Joel. "Are we there?"

The broomstick had come to a halt, hovering just a metre or so above a narrow strip of road, in the middle of a vast plain – at least, Gemma supposed it was a plain. She supposed it was a road. The road was deep purple, while the plain was a rather fetching pink, a bit like candy floss. Dotted all about it were long, skinny trees with bright green trunks and spiky leaves, with the odd little clump of bushes sprouting soft woolly balls every colour of the rainbow.

It was all very pretty, but just a little worrying. Gemma remained astride the broomstick, one leg hanging over the candy floss plain, the other over the purple road, not sure which side to jump off.

Joel, who never bothered to look before he leapt, was already knee deep in candy floss.

"I should be careful of that if I were you," began Ben-Muzzy, but his words of warning came too late. Even as Gemma watched, her twin went catapulting into the air, high over the tops of the long, skinny trees.

Good thing he's not scared of heights, thought Gemma.

"Hey! This is great!" cried Joel, coming back to earth with a great *boing!* into the candy floss and instantly setting off again. "Look! I can turn somersaults in mid-air!" He turned one. "It's like a – *boing!* – "trampoline – " *boing!* "You could – " *boing!* – "keep it up all – ooch! Ouch! That *hurt* – " as he came into contact with some of the sharp, spiky leaves – "all day!" *Boing!*

Gemma and Ben-Muzzy sat astride the hovering broomstick, watching as Joel bounced up and down.

"Showing off," said Gemma.

"Anyone could do it," said Ben-Muzzy, "if they felt like it."

Gemma wondered whether to join her twin but decided against it. It might be painful if you landed on the purple road instead of in the candy floss.

"Is that stuff safe?" she said, pointing.

"I'm not sure," said Ben-Muzzy. He waited hopefully for Gemma to try it. Gemma waited for Ben-Muzzy. And at that moment Joel obligingly went zooming past them, missed the candy floss, and landed with a flump on his patched backside.

"Interesting," said Joel, picking himself up. "Softer than it looks... I seem to have made a dent in it."

"Yes, and you've torn another hole in your jeans," said Gemma, delicately stepping off the broomstick. "And goodness, look what's happened!" she said. "That tree that you bashed into has started knitting!"

All the spiky leaves were busy clattering and clicking, casting on stitches as fast as they could go from the woolly balls that grew on the bushes. One by one, as Gemma watched, other trees began to join in, until very soon the whole plain was filled with the sound of clicking needles. There were trees knitting scarves, trees knitting socks, trees knitting sweaters in complicated patterns.

"That one's doing *Fair* Isle!" said Gemma. She stood, entranced. (Knitting was a mystery to Gemma. She could never work out which needle to poke through which loop, with the result that all her stitches tended to fall off in long strings, like frog-spawn.)

"That is totally, utterly brilliant!"

"Mum's not going to think it very brilliant

when she sees my jeans," grumbled Joel. She had told him only last week that "We're not made of money, you know." These jeans were supposed to have *lasted*.

"If you were a proper sort of wizard," he said to Ben-Muzzy, "you'd magic me a new pair."

"I'm not *made* of magic," said Ben-Muzzy, sounding for a moment just like Joel's mum. "I've got to keep what I have for when we find the witch."

"*If* we find the witch. Rate we're going – "

Heavens, they were off again!

"Why is the road this colour, do you suppose?" said Gemma.

"Why shouldn't it be?" said Joel.

Gemma couldn't really think of any answer to that. She supposed purple was as good a colour as the next.

The road was obviously not going anywhere in a hurry. It looped lazily round and about and among the skinny trees, but they had to keep to it if they didn't want to find themselves catapulting in and out of the candy floss.

After a while, it divided into two. They stood, undecided, not knowing whether to take the right fork or the left. Both of them were bright yellow.

"Ask him," said Gemma, as a piebald pony came trotting out of a nearby wood. If black cats could talk she didn't see any reason why ponies shouldn't be able to.

"Hey! Horse!" Joel capered after it. "Which way to the grungy witch?"

The pony stopped. "Did I hear someone mention witch?"

"Grungy witch that lives in a cave."
"The one that messes all her spells up?"
"That's the one!"
"Do you know her?" said Gemma.
"No, but I know someone that got turned

into a road by her."

"There! I told you," said Ben-Muzzy. "I told you she turned people into roads."

"If you've come thataway – " the pony waved a hoof at the purple road – "you'll have been walking on him."

Gemma turned pale. So that was why the road had been squidgy!

"Who was it?" she whispered.

"Oh, just some handsome prince she took a dislike to. Between you and me I think she fancied him, but he wasn't having any of it. Wanted to meet a beautiful princess. Which they always do," said the pony, "don't they? In the end? And then live happily ever after."

"Not if they've been turned into roads!" said Gemma. "Frogs and toads is what they're meant to be turned into. And then a beautiful princess comes along and kisses them. Who ever's going to kiss a road?"

"You can!" sniggered Joel. "That'd give him a nasty shock ... wake up and see you!"

Gemma was too used to her twin to notice the insult. If they ever managed to find this grungy witch, she was thinking, she would have to give her a good talking to. It was going against all the rules, turning handsome princes into roads. How could the poor man ever hope to meet his beautiful princess when he was just lying there being walked on? Especially as by now he must be squashed almost flat.

"Trust you," said Gemma.

"Me?" said Joel. "What have I done?"

"You've gone and put dents in him, that's what you've done! Bouncing about all over him. What kind of a princess," wailed Gemma, "wants a prince with dents? I think we'd better go and find this grungy witch *immediately*. Where is she? How do we get to her?"

"Either road will take you," said the pony, "but it's no use asking me how. I keep well away, myself; I've heard she has a bit of a nasty temper. Turn you into a black beetle as soon as look at you."

"She's not turning *me* into a black beetle," said Gemma.

Gemma went stomping off down one of the yellow roads. After a moment's hesitation, Joel and Ben-Muzzy followed. A dare was a dare, thought Ben-Muzzy. As for black beetles – he swished his cloak. She'd better not try any of that sort of nonsense with a wizard!

The yellow road wasn't quite as squidgy as the purple one had been, but Gemma trod cautiously all the same. She wouldn't like to think that she was bruising someone.

Rounding a corner, she came upon a furry Walloper filling his pouch with bits of twig. Wallopers loved to horde things: their pouches were always full of rubbish.

"Hello," said Gemma.

"Hilloo," said the Walloper. He peered down at her. "Does I know you?"

"You might do," said Gemma. "Did we meet just now?"

"Dunno," said the Walloper, tossing a couple of fir cones into his pouch. "Might have done. Might not have done. Can't tell really, can you?"

"No," agreed Gemma. "I suppose not."

Having no brain, Wallopers found it difficult to remember things; and since they all looked exactly alike it wasn't always possible to tell one from another.

"Anyway," said the Walloper, "it's been nice talking to you. I'll say cheerio now. Cheerio!"

"Oh, don't go!" said Gemma. "I want to ask you something."

The Walloper stopped.

"Hilloo!" it said. "Is that you again?"

"That's right," said Gemma. "We've just been talking."

"I thought we done." The Walloper nodded, proudly. "I thought I knows you. Well, I'll say cheerio, then. Cheerio! I'll be off, now."

"I don't suppose," said Gemma, hastily, "you've seen a soppy old witch living in a cave?"

"Soppy old witch living a cave ... soppy old witch living in a cave..." The Walloper scratched thoughtfully in an armpit. "Dunno about a soppy old witch. I know where there's a Smellibot. That do you?"

"Well, not really," said Gemma. It didn't seem very likely that a Smellibot would know where the witch was to be found, and even if it did she wasn't sure she could stand the stink long enough to ask it.

"Pity," said the Walloper, " 'cos I knows where to find one." He waved a paw. "Back there," he said. "Baby Smellibot. Blubbing."

"Blubbing?" said Gemma. "Why's it doing that?"

"Dunno. It's horrible. It smells."

"And it's crying? All by itself? A baby one? Oh, poor little thing!" cried Gemma. "It must be lost!"

"What's lost?" said Ben-Muzzy, who had just arrived with Joel.

"We are." Joel stated it glumly. He was beginning to think that this whole trip had been a mistake. "We might just as well get on the broomstick and go home."

"*No.*" Gemma stated it very firmly. "We're not going home till we've done what we set out to do."

"Well, I'm getting just about sick of it," said Joel. "I'd rather go back and play another trick on Graham Foster... We could send the broomstick down the chimney! That'd scare the socks off him!"

"We are not playing any more tricks on Graham Foster," said Gemma. "We're going to go and rescue a baby Smellibot. And *then* we're going to go and find the witch and get her to turn the handsome prince back into himself so that he can meet his beautiful princess and live happily ever after."

"You what?" said Joel.

"Do I have to repeat it?" said Gemma. "We are going to go and rescue a baby Smellibot – "

Joel swaggered. "Who says?"

"I do," said Gemma.

"She can't just boss us around like this," blustered Joel. He poked a finger at Ben-Muzzy. "Go on! Tell her! You're the one with the broomstick... Tell her!"

There was a pause.

"Um – " said Ben-Muzzy.

Gemma waited.

"Um – "

"Well?" said Joel.

"I'm the – ah – one with the – er – broomstick," said Ben-Muzzy.

"So what?" said Gemma.

"So – um – " Ben-Muzzy shot a nervous

glance at Joel. "So – ah – "

"Without the broomstick," prompted Joel, "she can't get home."

"Without the broomstick," bleated Ben-Muzzy, casting a piteous look at Gemma, "you can't get home."

"Oh, stop *blethering*!" said Gemma. "There's a poor little baby Smellibot, crying his eyes out. You can't just ignore him."

Joel and Ben-Muzzy both felt that in fact they could quite easily ignore him, but Gemma was really rather dreadful when she flew into one of her passions. Joel knew from experience that there was no arguing with her; she was just as likely to fly at him and start tearing his hair out. He dropped his eyes, scuffling with the toe of his trainer in a pile of leaves.

"Guess we'd better do what she wants," he muttered.

"Yes, yes!" Ben-Muzzy said it eagerly. "We'll do what she wants."

"And then," said Gemma, "we shall find the witch. *After* we've rescued the Smellibot."

"So where is this Smellibot?" said Joel, sulkily.

"He knows." Gemma prodded the

Walloper, still busy filling his pouch with bits and pieces. "Oy! You!"

The Walloper looked round. "Hilloo!" it said, surprised. "Does I know you?"

"Oh, now, don't start all that again!" begged Gemma. "I just want you to tell me where the Smellibot is."

"Smellibot?" The Walloper flared his nostrils. "What Smellibot?"

"The one you saw!"

"What one did I saw?"

(Joel said "Hah!" in tones of triumph.)

"You saw a little Smellibot, crying," said Gemma. You had to be patient with Wallopers. It wasn't their fault they had no brain.

"Back there." Gemma pointed. The Walloper chewed, blankly, on a length of stick.

"Maybe if we climbed into your pouch you could take us there," suggested Gemma. "Only we'd have to clean it out first," she said. "It's full of junk."

The Walloper held open his pouch and peered doubtfully inside.

"This, for instance – " Gemma hauled out a long strip of creeper. "You don't want that."

"Yes, I does!" The Walloper snatched at it and began stuffing it into his mouth.

"Well, then, *this*," said Gemma, distastefully removing an empty baked bean tin.

"I wants that!"

"What for?"

"Might come in useful."

It was a slow job, clearing out the Walloper's pouch. He was so reluctant to part with anything that in the end Gemma simply bundled all the nastiest, smelliest objects – the empty baked bean tin, the dead mouse, the rotting cabbage leaves – into an old string bag that she had found tucked away among the rubbish and slung it round the Walloper's neck. ("That's a good idea!" said the Walloper.) Gemma and Joel and Ben-Muzzy then clambered in and settled as comfortably as they could with their hands clinging to the edge of the pouch and their heads peering over the top. Every time one of them moved a foot, or even just twitched a toe, the Walloper giggled and said, "That tickles!" And every time the Walloper giggled they were thrown up and down and sideways until Gemma thought she might very probably be sick.

"Well, you asked for it," said Joel, watching as his twin turned first green and then yellow and secretly feeling that it would serve her right. Bossing them about like that! If she'd been a boy he wouldn't have let her, but girls, he sometimes thought, could get away with anything.

"You'd better just go one bound at a time," said Gemma, "otherwise we might miss it."

One thing Wallopers were good at was covering enormous stretches of ground at breakneck speed. Haaa-*whumpf!* went the Walloper, crashing through the undergrowth and dragging trails of greenery behind him.

It was on the third bound that they saw the Smellibot, tiny and forlorn, sitting on a tree stump, weeping most piteously. Its little pom-pom face was puckered, its big soft eyes

awash with tears. Around it, in a circle, were a crowd of Teeny Meanies, all prancing up and down going "Yuck!" and "Pooh!" and "Cor, what a pong!" as they jabbed at the Smellibot with their sharp pronged sticks.

"Stop! Stop!" cried Gemma.

The Walloper obligingly screeched to a halt (tearing the tops off a couple of trees as he did so). Gemma scrambled out of the pouch and went racing back to the Smellibot.

"Go away!" she shouted at the Teeny Meanies. "Leave him alone, you horrid creatures!"

All the Meanies rudely thumbed their noses at her as they slouched off, sniggering, into the woods. Gemma pulled out her handkerchief and pressed it to her face – the smell really was quite disgusting. Like bad drains and rotten eggs and stale kippers all mixed up into one enormous stink.

"What's the matter?" she said, bravely crouching down by the side of the weeping Smellibot. "Are you lost?"

Still weeping the Smellibot shook his head.

"So what is it?" said Gemma.

"I smell bad!" wept the Smellibot.

Gemma edged back a bit. The stink was

seeping through her handkerchief.

"Nobody loves me!" wept the Smellibot. "Nobody will talk to me!"

"Have you ever tried washing yourself?" said Gemma, trying to be kind but also stern, because really it was high time someone told him.

"I wash all the time," wept the Smellibot. "I wash and I wash and it won't go away!"

"Not even with soap?" said Gemma.

"Not even with soap!" wept the Smellibot.

Gemma was struck with a sudden rather terrible thought. Maybe this was how Smellibots were meant to smell? Maybe they were just naturally smelly creatures and there was nothing that could be done about it. But wouldn't you think, if that were the case, that they would be used to it?

"Have you always smelt this way?" she said, trying not to breathe too deeply.

"No!" Fresh spurts of tears rolled down the Smellibot's little frilly cheeks. If only he hadn't smelt so truly ghastly, thought Gemma, she would pick him up and cuddle him.

"It was the witch that done it to us!"

"The witch?" Gemma's ears pricked up.

"She cast an evil smell on us!"

From somewhere among the trees, where Joel and Ben-Muzzy were standing at a safe distance, came the sound of coarse guffawing.

"Oh, ho! Hee ha ho!" roared Joel and Ben-Muzzy, rolling about with their arms round each other.

"Tee hee! I told you she was always messing things up!"

"An evil smell!"

"Instead of an evil spell!"

"Oh, ho! He hee ho!"

"Stop laughing!" cried Gemma. "How would you like to have an evil smell cast on you? Don't take any notice of them," she told the Smellibot. "I'm afraid they are both rather childish. How long have you been like this?"

"Ages," wept the Smellibot.

"And are *all* of you like this?"

"Yes." The Smellibot nodded. "She said she was going to punish the whole lot of us."

"But why?" said Gemma. "What had you done?"

The Smellibot hung his head. "We laughed at her, 'cos she's always getting things wrong."

"Oh, I see. Well that *was* rather naughty, but all the same I don't think it's fair you should have to smell like this for the rest of your life. We must think what we can do."

"Can't do anything," the Smellibot wept afresh. "We're stuck like it for always."

"Nonsense," said Gemma. "My friend here is a wizard... He'll think of something."

She turned and beckoned to Joel and Ben-Muzzy. If she could put up with the stench, she didn't see why they couldn't.

"You heard what happened," she said to

Ben-Muzzy. "Your rotten old witch put an evil smell on him. You're a wizard. Take it away again!"

"I c-can't – " Ben-Muzzy was gasping, partly because of having laughed so much, and partly because of the rotten eggs and the drains and the stale kippers.

"What do you mean, you can't? Surely you've got a spell for removing other spells?"

"Not – w-witches' s-spells." Ben-Muzzy grabbed at a corner of his cloak and muffled his face in it. "Witches' – spells – only – removed – by – witches."

Gemma narrowed her eyes. "Is that true?"

"C-cross my c-cloak and hope to f-fly."

"In that case – " Gemma folded her arms – "there's only one thing for it. He'll have to come with us and see the witch."

"*No!*" Joel and Ben-Muzzy sprang backwards in horror. Gemma could rave and scream till she was blue in the face. She could tear out Joel's hair by the roots. She could spit and scratch and stamp and kick. They weren't going to go *anywhere* with a Smellibot.

"I'm not having it on the broomstick!" said Ben-Muzzy.

"He doesn't need to be on the broomstick. We're not *going* on the broomstick. We're going to find the witch."

"I've been thinking about that," said Ben-Muzzy. "What I've been thinking – "

What Ben-Muzzy had been thinking was that maybe he could go back to Podnock and *pretend* that he had seen the witch. Podnock would never know.

"I really don't care," said Gemma, "what you've been thinking. We came here to find the witch, and that is what we're going to do. There are wrongs," said Gemma, "that need to be righted. Come along!" She beckoned to the Smellibot. "But keep *behind*," she added, hastily.

"A long way behind," said Joel.

"A very long way," agreed the Walloper. "It's not getting in my pouch!"

They set off along the yellow road, Gemma in the lead, with Joel and Ben-Muzzy a few paces behind ("Always so *bossy*," Joel was grumbling), the Smellibot trailing, well in the rear, and the Walloper, who seemed to have attached itself to them, bounding all about them in big walloping circles. One minute he would be out of sight, the next landing with a

whumpf! at Gemma's side. Every time he landed he cried out in surprise, "Hilloo! That you again?" except once when he got it wrong and cried, "Hilloo! That me again?"

They walked on along the yellow road, round clumps of woolly bushes, until at last they came to a forest full of busily knitting trees. Gemma hesitated. The Walloper had gone walloping on. Joel and Ben-Muzzy came up behind and peered apprehensively into the depths of the forest. It was dark among the trees; they could just make out a narrow path winding through the thickets of stocking stitch and cable. The path was bright scarlet.

"What do we do?" said Joel.

"Um – well," said Ben-Muzzy.

"We follow the path!" said Gemma. There were wrongs that had to be righted.

Boldly, Gemma stepped foward, into the forest. The air was so full of knitting that it was impossible to walk without becoming entangled in it. Gemma found herself enveloped in the sleeves of a cardigan before she had realized what was happening. The cardigan instantly began to button itself round her.

"Hey! Stop it!" cried Gemma, but the cardigan just went on buttoning, *pop*, *pop*, *pop*, right up to the neck. "Help!" cried Gemma, clawing at the buttons. Now a woolly hat was knitting itself on to her head, tangling up her hair and using it to make bobbles.

"HELP!" roared Gemma, but Joel and Ben-Muzzy were fighting battles of their own. Joel was engaged in a tussle with a long, stripy scarf which had wound itself about his neck like a boa constrictor, while Ben-Muzzy was caught fast with his foot in a sock which refused to come off.

Panting and struggling Gemma fought to get out of the cardigan. As fast as she managed to undo one button and move on to the next, the first one promptly went and did itself up again. And all the time the woolly hat was steadily knitting itself into her hair, purling and plaining its way over her forehead, casting downwards over her eyes.

Desperately, Gemma wrenched at the cardigan, trying to yank the whole thing over her head. It wouldn't come off! Now she was stuck, her head smothered in cardigan, her arms still imprisoned in the sleeves. Gemma thrashed, wildly. Help me, somebody!

Nearby, the swaying tentacles of a pair of knitted stockings had noticed her plight. Eagerly, they lunged forward. One tentacle caught her round the throat, the other wrapped itself about her waist. Gemma felt the breath being slowly squeezed out of her. She felt herself being lifted off her feet and bundled up like a parcel. The tentacles writhed about her, round and round, until she was held fast in a cocoon, unable to move, scarcely able to breathe.

Gemma hung, helplessly, suspended in her cocoon. Just above her, though she couldn't see him, Joel was slung in the folds of the stripy scarf, while below, Ben-Muzzy was still wrestling to get out of his sock. Every time he managed to claw his way to the top, the sock simply added a few more rows of knitting to itself. It looked like a horrible furry slug with Ben-Muzzy wriggling inside it.

"Help!" cried Gemma; but no sound came out, and there was no one to hear it even if it had.

They were caught in the knitting, like flies in a spider's web. What would become of them?

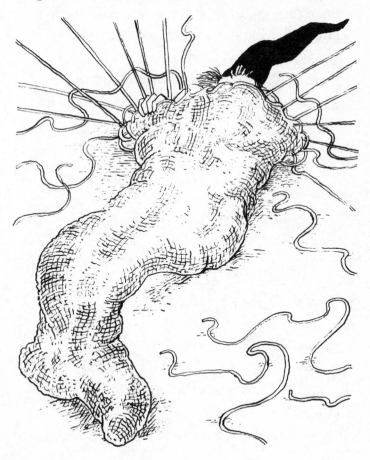

Maybe the witch would carry them off to her lair to cook in her cauldron. Nice roast twin, and boiled wizard with wurzels. Gemma could almost hear her thin, harsh, witchy voice: "I'll have one twin today, and one twin tomorrow ... keep the wizard for cold cuts."

I wish we'd never come! thought Gemma, desperately; but it was too late for wishing. They were caught in a trap of the witch's making.

How were they ever going to get out?

Chapter Seven

It was the Smellibot who rescued the twins
and Ben-Muzzy; the baby Smellibot, trailing
along behind, quietly grizzling to himself. As
he trundled into the forest, the terrible smell
of drains and stale cabbage trundled with
him. It rose about him in clouds. The knitting
trees faltered. The knitting needle leaves
began to curl at the edges. They began to
drop stitches one by one, and then in dozens,
until in the end whole rows were slipping off.
Garments were starting to unravel all over the
place. The stink was too much! The trees
couldn't take it. The witch had been too
clever for her own good.

Gemma found that the tentacles which held
her were slowly unwinding, slowly slipping
away, slithering through the strings of cast-off
stitches to the ground. The woolly hat, in a
panic, unwound itself; the cardigan shrivelled

and shrank. Gemma ripped it off like an old skin. She was free!

Joel dropped to his feet beside her.

"Where's Ben-Muzzy?"

"I'm here!" Ben-Muzzy was fighting his way out of the big furry slug of a sock.

"Quick! Run for it!"

The Smellibot had gone trundling on ahead. All the trees in his path were wilting; but already the ones behind were starting to recover, needles clicking back into action, casting on stitches, purling and plaining, making loops and bobbles as fast as they could go.

"Follow the smell!" cried Joel.

It was typical of Joel, thought Gemma, that even though it was the Smellibot who had saved them, he wasn't in the least bit grateful. He didn't say "Thank you" or "What a good job you were with us." All he did was peg his nose between finger and thumb and say, "Keeb away! I cahd dand de dink."

The Smellibot drooped. His little pom-pom face puckered.

"Oh, don't cry!" begged Gemma. "We're going to get something done for you. Just as soon as we find the witch ... you'll have to apologize, of course, and promise not to laugh at her again. And then you can ask her very nicely if she'd be so good as to remove the smell. From *all* of you. And I'm quite sure," said Gemma, "that she will."

"She won't!" sobbed the Smellibot. "We already asked her!"

"*What?*"

There was a stunned silence.

"You – you already *asked* her?" said Gemma.

"Yes." Tears went plopping down the pom-pom cheeks and rolling off the end of the little button nose. "She said we could go and get potted."

"Pardon?" said Gemma.

"She said, go and get potted!"

Knotted, thought Gemma; she must have meant knotted.

"Never mind what she said!" yelled Joel, suddenly springing to life and rushing forward (momentarily forgetting about the bad eggs and the drains). "You mean, you know where she lives?"

"Over there." The Smellibot pointed. "In a cave."

"Well, really!" said Gemma. "Why didn't you tell us before?"

"You never asked," said the Smellibot.

"Doesn't matter!" Joel did a victory roll. "We've found her!"

Only thanks to the Smellibot, thought Gemma.

Joel cackled, and biffed Ben-Muzzy on the shoulder. "Now we can go and have some fun! You can turn us back into black cats!"

"Not black cats." Ben-Muzzy had had enough of black cats.

"Well, something else, then!" Joel capered happily in a circle. "Let's get going! I want to find the grungy witch!"

They set off in a row, the Smellibot leading the way, with Gemma just behind, her nose buried in her handkerchief. The Walloper, who had suddenly reappeared, walloped along at Gemma's side, munching on a string of ivy, while Joel and Ben-Muzzy brought up the rear. From time to time either Joel or Ben-Muzzy would go "Phew!" or "Pong!" as the smell of eggs and drains and stale kippers wafted back to them.

"Look, just stop it, will you?" demanded Gemma, but Joel only made a vulgar gesture (Mum would have told him off had she been there) while Ben-Muzzy sniggered rather rudely. Ben-Muzzy's manners had become worse and worse since he had known Joel.

"Don't worry," said Gemma to the Smellibot, who had stopped weeping but was now sniffling to himself in a helpless sort of way. "We'll get the witch to put you right again."

She wasn't sure *how* she would get the witch to do this, but there had to be some way. To go round smelling like old kippers was a high price to pay for just having been a bit cheeky. If everyone that was a bit cheeky was made to smell bad, there simply wouldn't be any going anywhere *near* Joel. He wouldn't only smell of eggs and drains and kippers but of stagnant pools and dirty socks and garlic breath, as well.

The Smellibot shuffled across a tree-trunk bridge over a stream. The bridge wobbled dangerously as the twins and Ben-Muzzy set foot on it. The Walloper cleared it at a bound.

In the stream, flashing to and fro, were hundreds of brightly coloured fish. Some of the fish had their mouths open, showing rows of needle sharp teeth. Gemma had the uncomfortable feeling that they were lying in wait.

"They look like piranhas," said Joel; but piranhas weren't brightly coloured.

"More like a sort of goldfish," said Gemma. Goldfish with teeth.

"They're hers," said the Smellibot. "They were nice before she got at them." He wept afresh. "So were we! We were nice, too!"

"And you'll be nice again," promised Gemma. If the worst came to the worst, she thought, they could always take some of those tablets that her mum and dad took if they'd been eating onions and had to go out somewhere.

They followed the Smellibot into a tunnel through the undergrowth. The Smellibot was small enough to walk upright, but the twins and Ben-Muzzy had to crawl. (The Walloper had stayed behind to investigate a tasty-looking bush. When last seen he had been stuffing great wads of it into his pouch.)

On either side of the tunnel grew a long, spiky creeper with deep blue thorns that clutched and clawed.

"Ow!" yelped Gemma, as one snatched at her hair.

The thorns were tougher than the knitting trees: they didn't wilt as the Smellibot trundled through.

"It was her that put them there," said the Smellibot. "She doesn't like people coming to visit."

"She sounds extremely anti-social," said Gemma, disapprovingly.

"Witches are," muttered Ben-Muzzy.

"Well, she'll have to be taught a lesson! She can't – ouch! – be allowed to carry on – *ow!* – like this."

"We'll teach her a lesson all right!" crowed Joel.

"Several lessons," urged Ben-Muzzy.

Now that at last their goal was in sight, they had become rather cocky.

"Spell-or-Spill!" crowed Ben-Muzzy. Wait until he got back and told Podnock about this! Podnock had only flown over on a broomstick: Ben-Muzzy was about to enter the actual lair.

Pricked, scratched and torn, they crawled out of the end of the tunnel and found themselves in a small clearing in the middle of the woods.

"Over there," said the Smellibot, lifting up a paw. "That's where she lives ... behind those prickle things."

The twins and Ben-Muzzy, with the Smellibot padding after them, crept across the clearing and crouched down behind the prickle things. (The prickle things were capable of giving you a nasty jab, as Gemma quickly discovered. They had leaves like spikes and egg-shaped berries like miniature hand grenades. Maybe they *were* hand grenades. The witch seemed willing to go to quite extraordinary lengths to keep people out.)

The Smellibot was crouching rather closer to Gemma than Gemma would have liked, but it would have been unkind to move away. She would just have to try not to breathe too deeply. Joel and Ben-Muzzy were crouched together, at a distance. They were elbowing and nudging at each other, pulling silly faces.

"That's her," said the Smellibot.

Gemma peered cautiously, trying to keep her face well away from the spike-shaped leaves.

There, at the entrance to her cave, was the grungy witch. She didn't look nearly as scary as Joel and Ben-Muzzy had done when they were frightening Graham Foster; in fact, she looked rather mad and messy. Her hair was full of tangles, and bits of branch and twig. Her tall steeple hat was battered and bent and had slipped sideways, her black witch's cloak covered in stains and frayed at the edges. Round her neck hung a pair of pink plastic spectacles on a piece of string.

"Double, double, boil and bubble," chanted the witch, stirring at something in a dented cauldron.

"Look at that!" whispered Ben-Muzzy. "A wizard would be ashamed to own a cauldron in that state."

"Sh!" hissed Gemma. "She'll hear you."

For a dreadful moment Gemma thought that the witch had indeed heard them, for her head jerked up, toppling her hat even further sideways, and her yellow eyes narrowed.

"What's that?" she said.

There was a great crashing among the trees and the Walloper came walloping in. (Gemma could tell that it was *their* Walloper from the remains of a string bag that was hanging

round his neck.) Without waiting for an invitation, the Walloper went bounding up to the cauldron and dunked his nose into it.

"What's cooking, good looking?"

"Here! You watch what you're doing!" screeched the witch. "That's my smell you're interfering with!"

"Ugh! Tastes nasty," said the Walloper, removing his nose from the cauldron.

"It's a nasty sort of smell," said the witch.

"You can say that again," agreed the Walloper. He looked at the witch, reproachfully. "It wasn't very nice."

"It wasn't meant to be!" snapped the witch.

"What you got in here?" Nothing daunted – Wallopers were really quite unsquashable, especially in pursuit of food – the Walloper walloped across to the cave and peered in with big baggy eyes. "This looks all right! What's this?"

He dipped his paw into a bowl and pulled out a handful of spotted jelly.

"You leave that alone! That's my fog sprawn. Give it back!" The witch made a lunge at him. As she did so, she tripped over a large marmalade cat, stretched out lazily on the ground.

"Oh, get out of the way, you great lumping thing!" The witch gave a shriek as the spotted jelly disappeared down the Walloper's throat. "You've gone and eaten my prog spawn! I wanted that for a smell!"

"Mm." The Walloper licked his lips. "Not bad. What else you got?"

"Nothing for the likes of you," snapped the witch. She peered testily at the Walloper's identification disc. (All Wallopers had identification discs in case they forgot who they were.) "What's that say?" She thrust her pink plastic spectacles on her nose. "Great Furry Plonker?"

"Illiterate," hissed Joel.

He should talk, thought Gemma. Joel had a reading age of about *two*.

"Walloper," said the Walloper. He scratched his ear. "I think."

"I'll wallop you if you don't get out! I'm in the middle of a very important spell, I mean smell, I mean – well, whatever it is, I'm in the middle of it, so push off!"

"All right." The Walloper furtled cheerfully in his pouch. "If you've got no grub, I'll say goodbye and cheerio!"

"And good riddance," grumbled the witch, going back to her smell. "Where was I?" She picked up her long, bent-handled spoon and began swishing again in the cauldron.

Joel and Ben-Muzzy exchanged glances. Ben-Muzzy raised an eyebrow and pointed to his hat; Joel nodded. Ben-Muzzy took the hat off and tossed it into the air.

"At the count of number three... "

Resolutely, Gemma turned her back on them. Them and their stupid pranks! She was more interested in watching the witch.

"*Double, double, boil and* wotsisname," chanted the witch, agitating her spoon. "And wotsisname, and wotsisname," she added, forgetting her lines.

Nearby, the marmalade cat sat washing itself on a big fat book. The witch prodded at it with the tip of a bony finger.

"Shift yourself! That's my book of smells, I mean spells, I mean – oh, get off of it!"

The cat, with a resigned expression, removed itself and went to stretch out in the entrance to the cave. The witch opened her book, licked a finger and began leafing through the pages.

"Now, let's see..." She rammed her spectacles on to her nose. The spectacles promptly slipped down to the end of it. The witch shunted them up again: the spectacles slipped down again. Up, down, up, down, went the spectacles. There wasn't any glass in them, anyway.

"*Double, double,*" muttered the witch, tracing the words with her finger. "*Double, double, and* wotsisname ... and wotsisname ... and something or other – "

No wonder she kept getting her spells wrong, thought Gemma. No one had ever taught her how to read properly.

"Oh, bother!" screamed the witch, losing patience. She slammed the book shut and let her spectacles fall off her nose. "I'll do another one!"

She went back to the cauldron and began stirring frantically. Blobs of greasy liquid went splattering over her cloak.

"It's not gluggy enough," complained the witch. "I can't get it gluggy enough. That's your fault, that is!" She turned to the cat. "Useless great lump!"

The cat stared at her, unblinking.

"You're supposed to help me! You're supposed to be my familiar! Fat lot of good you are, just sitting there!"

The cat yawned, and curled up into a ball.

"That's right!" screeched the witch. "You have a good sleep. Don't mind me!"

She snatched up a handful of leaves and gunge and flung it into the cauldron.

"Scum and matter pie, fit to make you die, and a cup of cold sick – where's my cold sick? What's happened to my cold sick? What's this?"

She clawed up an old saucepan without any handle and sunk her long, pointy nose into it.

"This isn't sick. What is it? Whatever it is, it'll have to do."

The contents of the saucepan went slopping

and slurping into the cauldron. A great mess of gluggy bubbles at once rose up and gurgled over the side.

"That's better! Now we're getting somewhere... *Creepy crawly, snakey slime, sticky stumps and grolly grime, bane of rat and spongy toes, bone of –* "

The witch stopped, and ran over to her book of spells.

"Bone of ... bone of what?" She put her spectacles back on, clamping them in place with one finger, and peered closer. "Hat? Mat?"

"Bat, I should think," said Gemma, before she could stop herself.

"Who said that?" The witch spun round, bumping into the cauldron as she did so. The cauldron promptly tipped over, spilling a dark green gluggy mess across the ground. The witch screamed and shook her fist.

"Whoever you are, I'll put a smell on you! I'll condemn you to everlasting wotsisname! I'll cast a smell that will make you squirt – squint— "

"Squirm?" suggested Gemma.

"One more creak out of you," raged the witch, "and I'll – I'll turn you into a wet dishcloth!"

She rushed towards the bushes, where Gemma and the Smellibot were crouching.

"Where are you?" panted the witch.

Gemma shrank back into the shadows. She didn't know whether to laugh or whether to turn and run, but in any case the Smellibot, terrified, had suddenly hurled himself at her and was clutching her round the middle with little smelly paws.

"Don't let her get me! Don't let her get me!"

In spite of the bad eggs and the drains, Gemma hadn't the heart to unclasp him.

"I can hear you!" screamed the witch. "I'll teach you to mock at me! I'll pull your teeth out by the roots! I'll make your hair rot! I'll melt your eyeballs! I'll turn your lips frizzy! I'll— "

What else she would have done, Gemma never knew, for at that moment the sky drew dark, there was a loud rumbling of thunder, and overhead, riding the switchback of a jagged streak of lightning, appeared a broomstick and two hideous figures.

The Smellibot screamed and buried his face in Gemma's T-shirt.

"It's all right," said Gemma, soothingly. "It's only Joel and Ben-Muzzy."

The two horrible hags rode again, blood-
red eyes, horny fingernails, long, thin noses
with points as sharp as darning needles. Their
cackles and curses filled the air as the
broomstick slipped off the edge of the
switchback and zoomed over the tops of the
trees.

At the entrance to the cave, the marmalade
cat sat watching: the cat wasn't fooled for one
moment. But the witch was. Helter skelter she
ran, from the bushes to the cave, from the
cave to the cauldron, holding out her arms to

the figures on the broomstick.

"Oh, dearest ones, you've come, you've come! At last you've come! Oh, I've waited for this day! Take me back with you, don't leave me here! Everybody hates me – everybody laughs at me! I'm lonely! I'm so lonely! Oh, dearest ones, I beseech you – "

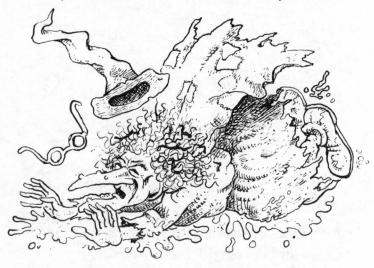

At this point the witch slipped in the pool of green glug and tripped, headlong. Her hat fell off, her glasses scrunched. She staggered, sobbing, to her feet.

"I'll do better – I'll try harder! I'll get my smells right!"

From the broomstick came two jeering cackles of laughter. One of the figures actually put its bony fingers to its pointy nose and splayed them. *Joel*, thought Gemma.

"Oh, please!" The witch's voice rose in a wail. Her hair hung in tatters, her cloak was soiled and shredded. Gemma felt almost sorry for her. Even the Smellibot had turned his head to watch.

"Take me back with you! I beg of you!"

"We wouldn't take you back if you were the last witch left on earth!" taunted one of the hags.

"Grungy old bag!" added the other.

Really, thought Gemma, *this is too much*. A joke was a joke, but it wasn't fair to humiliate a person like this, not even if she *was* a witch. Not even if she *had* turned a handsome prince into a purple road and put an evil smell on the little pom-pom creatures. Gemma could quite understand that if everyone kept laughing at you and rejecting your advances, which was what the handsome prince had done, you would feel like turning them into roads and putting smells on them. It couldn't be allowed to continue, of course; but sneering and jeering was no way to stop it.

What the witch needed, thought Gemma,

was someone to talk to her kindly and sensibly, but also *firmly*, and help her see the error of her ways. Poking fun at her would only make matters worse.

It already had made matters worse. Suddenly realizing that she had been tricked, and that the two hideous hags on the broomstick were not fellow witches at all, the witch gave an immense shriek of rage, rushed into the depths of her cave (falling over the cat yet again) and came flying out astride a broomstick of her own.

"Abracadabra toads' feet and newt!" screamed the witch, soaring into the air.

Now they'll cop it, thought Gemma. The witch might not be too clever at doing spells, but she certainly knew how to fly a broomstick. Witches were brought up speaking broomstick language; it was second nature to them.

"Meht teg! Meht pots! Yawa teg meht tel tnod!"

Ben-Muzzy was simply no match for her. Talking backwards had never been his strong point.

Gemma and the Smellibot – the Smellibot with his little smelly paw tucked into

Gemma's hand – stood watching as the broomsticks swooped and circled. The witch's broomstick was far faster than Ben-Muzzy's; it was obviously a later model. Joel and Ben-Muzzy floundered helplessly to and fro, crashing into trees and dangerously skimming the tops of bushes. And all the time the witch was shouting out her instructions – *"Meht mar! Ffo meht daeh! Nwod meht ecrof!"*

The broomstick responded magnificently. This was *real* broomstick control, thought Gemma.

"Nwod! Nwod! Ereht revo! Nwod!"

And then Gemma saw what she was trying to do: she was trying to force them to land in the stream full of the goldfish-piranhas, with their rows of waiting teeth. They would make short work of Joel and Ben-Muzzy. Gemma rushed frantically out into the open.

"Ben-Muzzy!" she yelled. "Watch out! Tell the broomstick to keep away!"

She knew which one Ben-Muzzy was, because he was the hag that was operating the broomstick. She could see him struggling to work out "keep away" in broomstick talk, but fortunately the unexpected appearance of a twin from out of the bushes had momentarily broken the witch's concentration. Hastily, Gemma counted backwards on her fingers.

"*Yawa peek!*" she shouted. "*Yawa peek!*"

The witch whipped her broomstick round in a tight circle.

"*Meht mar! Meht mar! Maerts eht otni!*"

The witch's broomstick did its best, but already the two horrible hags, saved by Gemma's quick thinking, were coming in to land.

"Hurry!" Dragging the broomstick with one hand, the hag that was Ben-Muzzy seized Gemma with the other. (Gemma flinched, in spite of knowing that it was only Ben-Muzzy.) "Find some oak trees! Quick!"

Too late: the witch, also, had landed.

"By the power of the broomstick – " she pointed at them, with quivering finger – "reveal yourselves in your true forms or go to everlasting wotsisname!"

There was a puff of smoke, and the two hideous hags disappeared.

Gemma waited, anxiously. How could she go home and tell her mum and dad that Joel had gone to everlasting wotsisname? (How could she go home, without Ben-Muzzy and the broomstick?)

"Well, come on!" snapped the witch. "Don't take all day! Let's have a look at you."

There was another puff of smoke and to Gemma's relief Ben-Muzzy and her twin stepped out of it, restored to their normal selves and looking rather sheepish.

"Oh, so it was you, was it?" screeched the witch, glaring at Ben-Muzzy. "You, playing tricks on me! I might have known it! I shall report you to the Grand High Lizard! I shall— "

"But it's All Spells' Night," protested Ben-Muzzy. "You know we always play tricks on All Spells' Night!"

"I'll play a trick or two on you, you ill-mannered lizard! I'll turn you into a hat, I mean mat, I mean – oh, drat it, I'll turn you into frogs' legs, I'll – " She peered short-sightedly at her book of spells. "I'll do something else, as well!"

"Oh, now, look here," said Ben-Muzzy, "surely we can talk about this?"

"I don't want talk, I want action!" The witch picked up the book and hurled it. Then she turned and went sprawling over the cat. "Get out of my way, you useless lump!"

"You ought to be ashamed of yourself, talking to a cat like that," said Ben-Muzzy.

"I'll talk to it how I like! Don't you think you can come here, laying down the floor! I'm sick of you, you stupid lizard. I've a good mind to put a hearse on you!"

Joel sniggered. "She means curse."

"I mean what I mean! And since you think it's so funny – " the witch spun round to Joel – "I'll put one on you, as well!"

Chapter Eight

With a roar and a whoosh and a loud squeal of brakes, a big black shiny car landed on top of Ben-Muzzy's head. On top of Joel's landed another. Both cars had the words FUNERAL DIRECTOR printed along the side.

There was a silence. The smile slowly faded from Joel's lips.

"W-what's happened?" he said. He put up a hand, to feel. "Wh-what is it?"

"A hearse," said Gemma, "I suppose."

"That'll teach them," sniggered the witch; but even she sounded a trifle uncertain.

"You didn't mean to put a hearse on them, did you?" said Gemma. "You meant to put a curse."

"I meant what I meant." The witch said it sullenly. She obviously didn't like to admit that she muddled up her words. It had been the same with a boy in Gemma's class at

school; he hadn't wanted to admit it, but in
the end he had had to and now he was having
special reading lessons and could read almost
as well as anybody else. That was what the
witch needed: reading lessons.

Ben-Muzzy cleared his throat.

"That was a very good trick," he said.
"Very funny. I enjoyed it. But I've had enough
of it now, so if you'd just very kindly like to
remove it – "

The witch sniffed.

"It's getting," said Joel, "rather *heavy*."

"Too bad," said the witch. "You're stuck like it now."

The witch flounced away, to pick up her overturned cauldron. Joel swivelled his eyes as best he could in Ben-Muzzy's direction.

"Do something!" he said.

"I can't," said Ben-Muzzy. "I told you ... only a witch can undo a witch's curse."

"But it isn't a curse, it's a hearse!"

"Comes to the same thing," muttered Ben-Muzzy.

"Exactly." With an air of satisfaction, the witch began pouring water into her cauldron from an old tin kettle. The marmalade cat sat watching her. "Curse, hearse ... it's all the same."

"Now, you know that isn't true," said Gemma, reproachfully. "A curse isn't at *all* the same thing as a hearse. Any more than a purse is. Any more than a – than a *nurse* is. They're all quite different."

The witch sulked.

"Get this off of me!" roared Joel, rolling his eyes to and fro. (The hearse was too heavy for him to move his head.)

The witch tossed a handful of deadly nightshade into the cauldron.

"Why should I?"

"Because – " Gemma said it gently: it wasn't the least bit of use shouting and bellowing – "because it was a *mistake*. Wasn't it?"

The witch hunched a shoulder.

"Just like it was a mistake when you put an evil smell on the Smellibots. Just like it was when you turned the handsome prince into a road."

"Hah!" The witch rummaged triumphantly in a bowl of mouldy fungus. "Served him right."

"But how much better," said Gemma, "if you'd done what you meant to do and turned him into a toad."

"Oh, I don't know," said the witch, dropping bits of mouldy fungus into the cauldron. "I should say it does him good to be trodden on for a change."

"But don't you see?" said Gemma. "This is why people laugh at you. It's why you were sent into exile, isn't it? Because you keep turning people into the wrong thing."

The witch's withered white cheeks became rather hot and red when Gemma said this. She threw down her bowl of fungus and snatched up a dead rat instead.

"Imagine," said Gemma, "if someone were to teach you how to read properly – "

"It's nothing to do with reading properly. I can read as well as anyone. It's that useless fat lump over there!" The witch flung her dead rat at the cat. The cat didn't even bat an eyelid. "Look at it! It's supposed to be helping me. All it ever does is sleep."

"That's because it's the wrong colour," jeered Ben-Muzzy. "Whoever heard of a witch with a marmalade cat?"

"They wouldn't let me have a black one." The witch stuck her long-handled spoon into the cauldron and began to stir, rather viciously. Liquid slopped and splashed over the side. "They said it would be a waste. They said— "

"Excuse me," said Gemma. "Don't you think you ought to wear a pinny if you're going to start cooking things?"

Gemma walked into the cave to look for one. The cave was even messier than the witch herself; Gemma had never seen anywhere so untidy – and *she* had seen Joel's bedroom. At least Joel's bedroom didn't have piles of dead rats lying around. At least it didn't have a compost heap mouldering in the middle of it, or shelves full of bottles and jars all higgledy piggledy, with half their contents spilling out, or great bulging cobwebs full of rotting insects, or creepers strung across the ceiling.

"This place is a *pig*sty!" said Gemma, snatching at a dirty grey towel that was hanging from a creeper. She marched back out. Joel and Ben-Muzzy had sunk down beneath the weight of their hearses and were sitting glumly side by side. The witch was mumbling over her cauldron.

"*Wing of hat and eye of nude –* "

"Newt," said Gemma. "And wing of bat. Put this round yourself, please – and let us have no arguments! Everyone has to wear a pinny when they're cooking."

"Never mind the pinny!" shouted Joel. "What about us?"

"I'm afraid you'll just have to stay as you are for the moment," said Gemma. It wouldn't hurt them, and anyway they had brought it on themselves. "I'll see to you later. We have other things to do first."

"Go away," said the witch. "Stop interrupting me. I'm working on a smell."

"Spell," said Gemma.

"You keep out of it!" the witch. "How do you know it's not a smell?"

"That's right," muttered Joel. "Bossy old bat."

Gemma turned on him.

"You'd better be quiet," she said, "if you don't want to spend the rest of your life with a hearse on you." She turned back to the witch. "Where's your book of smells? I mean – " hastily, she corrected herself – "I mean, spells. Is this it?"

"Not telling you," said the witch.

"Well, I can see that it is," said Gemma. "It says on it ... *First Booke of Spelles.*"

Ben-Muzzy tittered. "She's still on the first book!"

"It's not mine!" said the witch. "It's someone else's. I only use it for throwing at the cat."

"A likely tale!" scoffed Ben-Muzzy.

The witch began to grow rather hot and red again.

"Oh, now, please," begged Gemma. "You mustn't let Ben-Muzzy upset you. I remember when we first met him he'd just gone and lost himself on account of using the wrong magic. *And* I remember when he produced a pink elephant out of a hat instead of a rabbit."

"Pink elefump?" The witch threw back her head and cackled, happily. "Stupid lizard!"

"Wizard," said Gemma. She opened the book.

" 'Spelle for Transforming Prince or Princesse into Frogge or Toade,' " read Gemma.

> "At dead of night, beneath ye full gaze of ye midsummer moone, sally ye forth unto the hedgerowes and there garner unto yourselfe one winge of batte, one lengthe of

worme, two goodly sprigges of the plant
belladonna and as many cockroache,
blacke beetle and slugge as may be found,
alle to be left soaking in a bowle of
stagnante water covered with noxious
scumme and to which for assured success
add three droppes of ye hennebane and stirre."

"Yes. Well, all right, then," said Gemma, a
trifle doubtfully. "See what you can do with
that."

"It's all nonsense!" cried the witch. "I work
from memory!"

"Like bubble, bubble boil and
wotsisname," said Gemma. "It's no wonder
your spells go wrong. Look, wouldn't you
like to be able to read?" She could see that
the witch was tempted. "How about this, for
instance?"

Gemma broke a twig off one of the bushes
and wrote with it in the earth: THE CAT SAT ON
THE MAT. The witch considered it, frowning.

"What does that say?" said Gemma.

"The mat – sat on the bat?" said the witch,
hopefully.

Gemma shook her head.

"The bat sat on the mat?"

"Now, work it out," said Gemma. "You're

not trying. C-A-T spells – "

"Cat!" The witch's face lit up. "The cat sat on the hat! That great lump over there sits on hats. That's why mine is all crushed out of shape. It's supposed to sit on my shoulder, but of course," said the witch, bitterly, "it never does."

"It would if it were a black one!" shouted Ben-Muzzy.

"Just think," urged Gemma, "if you learnt to read you could probably say a spell that would turn it into a black one ... M-A-T spells mat, by the way; not hat."

"The cat sat on the mat?"

Gemma nodded.

The witch leapt up and punched the air exultantly with a gnarled fist. "The cat sat on the mat! The cat sat on the mat! I've got it, I've got it!"

"You're starting to get it," agreed Gemma. "But that's only the beginning. You still couldn't read about transforming princes into toads, could you?"

She held out the *First Booke of Spelles*, open at page one.

"You'd still do something stupid like turning them into roads, wouldn't you?" The witch put a horny fingernail into her mouth and chewed at it. "Now, I *could* teach you how to read it," said Gemma, "and then you'd be able to change all the princes you liked into frogs or toads, just as you wanted, *and* you'd be able to turn your cat into a black one. *And* all your spells would go right so that people wouldn't laugh at you any more. *But* – "

Gemma paused. The witch took her fingernail out of her mouth.

"But what?" she said.

"You'd have to promise me a few things."

"What things?"

"First you'd have to promise you'd put my twin and our wizard friend back the way they were before."

The witch cast a withering look at Joel and Ben-Muzzy. (They were now slumped with their backs against a tree trunk.)

"One stupid lizard and an idiotic toy?" she sneered. "It hardly seems worth it."

"Wizard," said Gemma. "And boy."

"Still doesn't seem worth it."

"Look, are you going to promise or— "

"Oh, all right! If I must."

"Don't trust her!" yelled Joel. "Get her to put us back first!"

Gemma hesitated. You had to trust people sometimes; and it would be good for the witch to feel that she was being treated as a responsible being for once, instead of some grungy old failure that everyone laughed at.

"I'm sure if she promises, she'll keep her word," said Gemma, "won't you?" And in honeyed tones, she added, "What is your name, by the way?"

"Grimwade," said the witch.

"Grimwade!" said Gemma. "What a beautiful name! May I call you Grim?"

"No," said the witch.

"Oh. Well. All right, then, Grimwade. The second thing you've got to promise is that you'll remove the smell from the Smellibots. There is a little Smellibot over there," said Gemma, pointing to where a small anxious pom-pom face could be seen peering through the bushes, "who's been made very unhappy by you putting a smell on him."

"Hah! That'll teach him to laugh at me."

"Well, I'm sure it *has* taught him. But by the time I've helped you learn to read and you've carried out your promises, there won't be any reason for anyone to laugh at you, will there? So do you promise to remove the smell?"

"Oh, I suppose," said the witch.

"Good! Because there's only one more promise I want you to make and that's that you'll turn the handsome prince back into a handsome prince, before so many people walk on him that he gets squashed completely flat."

Gemma had thought she might have trouble with this one, especially if the prince had spurned the witch's advances, but Grimwade only gave another of her cackles and said, "Oh, I don't mind doing that... I'll turn him back into being a handsome prince. Much good will it do him!"

"Why?" said Gemma.

Grimwade looked sly. "Not telling you."

"But you do promise you'll turn him back?"

"She said so!" roared Joel. "Just get on with it!"

"Very well." With the toe of her trainer Gemma rubbed out THE CAT SAT ON THE MAT and in its place, with her pointed stick, wrote: THE BLACK CAT HELPS THE GOOD WITCH.

"Now, then," said Gemma.

Gemma was enjoying herself. She sometimes thought that when she grew up she might quite like to be a teacher; it was fun bossing people around and telling them what to do.

"How long is she going to take?" hissed Ben-Muzzy.

Joel tried to shake his head and found that he couldn't: the hearse had pressed it right down between his shoulders. He watched, gloomily, as Gemma and Grimwade squatted together on the ground.

"B-L-A-C-K," Gemma was saying, as she

moved Grimwade's bony finger along the line of words.

"I think my head is disappearing," said Ben-Muzzy.

"I think mine is, too," said Joel.

It was true: both their heads were sinking lower and lower into their bodies. Their necks had already gone; it was only a matter of time before first their chins, and then their mouths, and then their noses followed suit. How would they be able to breathe when their noses were gone?

"Help!" bleated Joel and Ben-Muzzy as their chins slowly descended between their shoulders.

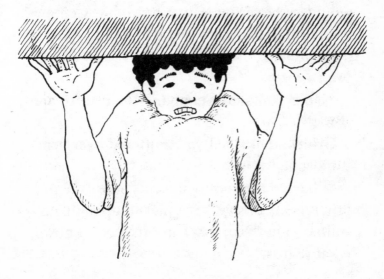

"Help!" they gurgled, as their mouths began to sink out of sight.

"He-e-e-e— "

Their cries were cut short. Their mouths had gone! Gemma looked at them, rather irritably. What a nuisance they were! Grimwade had just started to read the spell for transforming princes and princesses, and was doing rather well.

"Oh, all right," said Gemma. "I suppose we'll have to stop there. You'd better do something to those two before they lose their heads entirely."

There were some people – Graham Foster, for one – who might have said that Joel would be better without a head, but Gemma didn't think her mum and dad would like it too much. *This is our son without any head – "*

"Quickly!" said Gemma. "Their noses are going!"

Grimwade turned and muttered over her cauldron.

"I'll need a pot of warts... Where's me pot of warts? Is this it?" She picked up a jug and sniffed at it. "No, that's not it. Don't know what that is."

"*Hurry!*" urged Gemma.

"Oh, well, I'll put this in and see what happens... Double, double, boil and bubble, remove the curse and all its trouble... It's not nearly as much fun as putting curses *on* people. And oh, dear!" said Grimwade. "There they are, back again. How horrible! They looked much nicer when their heads had gone. Are you sure you want them back? I could easily put another hearse on them."

"You'd better *hadn't*!" said Ben-Muzzy.

"Why not, you stupid lizard? I mean wizard. You mend your manners or I'll turn you into something nasty."

"Now, look here," said Gemma, "we don't want any more of this. Not from either of you. Magic powers," said Gemma, "ought to be used *sensibly*."

"Killjoy," muttered Joel, though truth to tell he had had a bit of a fright when he had thought his entire head was going to disappear.

All that remained now was for Grimwade to remove the smell from the Smellibots and restore the handsome prince to his handsome self. After a bit of pottering and fussing over the cauldron, and running distractedly in search of magic ingredients – "Where's me tansy? Where's me teasle? I've looked in every hook and granny!" – she finally found the spell for removing smells.

"All right," she said. "Where is he?"

They could tell where the Smellibot was from a cloud of flies, hovering above the bushes.

"Let him come fifth," commanded Grimwade.

"You mean forth," said Gemma.

"I mean what I mean! Fourth, fifth, where's the difference? Come out of those bushes!"

A bashful Smellibot padded forward, the flies buzzing at his backside.

"Pooh! What a stink!" cried Grimwade, fanning the air with her pinafore.

"Well, you were the one that put it there," said Gemma. "Just get on with the spell! And remember, you've got to do it for *all* of them, not just our one."

Muttering to herself, Grimwade made a series of passes over the cauldron. A plume of dirty brown smoke rose into the air. The stench was so dreadful that Gemma and Grimwade both staggered backards, choking. Joel clamped his fingers to his nose, Ben-

Muzzy smothered his face in his cloak. Even the marmalade cat twitched a nostril.

"That is disgusting!" gasped Gemma.

"Best smell I ever made." Grimwade seemed quite proud of herself. She picked up a tattered piece of blanket and wafted it to and fro over the cauldron. "You did say all of them."

Well, yes, thought Gemma; that was only fair. You couldn't just remove the smell from one and not the others.

When the smoke had cleared and she could breathe again Gemma turned to the Smellibot.

"Let me smell you," she said.

Shyly, the Smellibot presented himself for inspection. Gemma sniffed the air, cautiously. She moved a bit closer and sniffed some more.

"It's gone!" She threw her arms about him and hugged him. "You're not a Smellibot any more! You're a Sweetibot!"

Joel groaned. The Sweetibot went gambolling joyfully off into the sunshine, leaving a trail of disgruntled flies behind him. They would never find a smell as lovely as that one!

"Well," said Gemma, in tones of satisfaction, "that was a g— "

She broke off as a gang of Teeny Meanies suddenly burst in wearing stripy scarves and big boots and waving wooden rattles.

"Ya, ya, stupid old witch!" chanted the Teeny Meanies. "Can't get her spells right, stupid old witch!" Then they caught sight of Ben-Muzzy, whose tall wizard's hat had been crushed almost flat by the hearse. "Dopey old wizard, look at the state of him! Look at his hat! Squashed flat!"

With one accord, Ben-Muzzy and Grimwade rushed at them.

"One more creak out of you..." snapped Grimwade.

"...and we'll turn you into black beetles!" shouted Ben-Muzzy.

The Teeny Meanies ran off, tittering and waving their rattles.

"You just wait," said Grimwade, "I'll get them!"

"Not before you've restored the prince," said Gemma.

"Oh, yes! Him. Let's get him back and see what he looks like. Where's me bats' wings? What did I do with me bats' wings?"

The bats' wings were found and tossed into the cauldron. A coil of smoke rose into the air, carrying the bats' wings with it. Smoke and wings drifted off in the direction of the purple road.

"Wait for it," snickered Grimwade. "Here he comes!"

The smoke eddied back, whirling in a spiral, propelled by the bats' wings. From the middle of it stepped a handsome prince. He was a *very* handsome prince, dressed in a purple doublet with yellow hose and scarlet boots, and a big purple hat with a scarlet feather.

"Oh, wow!" breathed Gemma. She could see why Grimwade had fancied him.

"How do you feel," said Joel, with interest, "after being a road for so long?"

"A trifle bruised," said the Prince, "but otherwise not too bad." He set his hat at a jaunty angle and slapped a hand against his princely thigh. "Now to find my Princess!"

"He'll be lucky," giggled Grimwade, as the Prince strode manfully off in his purple boots.

"Why?" Gemma looked at her, sharply. "You've done something to her! What have you done?"

"Nothing that she didn't deserve. Bumptious cow! Always looking at herself in the mirror, thinking how beautiful she was... I settled her hash! I made a spell for turning her plain. Only thing was, something went

wrong and she turned *into* a plain, instead. Oh, I did laugh!"

"Hey! You don't mean she's that candy floss stuff?" said Joel.

"Yes!" Grimwade doubled over, clutching her ribs. "*Up,* down, *up,* down ... bumpity bump – " Grimwade collapsed, wheezing, by the side of her cauldron. "That'll have knocked some of the stuffing out of her!"

"It was like being on a trampoline," said Joel.

"Bumpity bump... I told you she was bumptious!"

"Oh, now, really! This is too bad," said Gemma. "You can just jolly well bring her back again!"

"Shan't," said Grimwade. "Don't like her."

"Look, there isn't any point in being jealous," said Gemma, "just because she's beautiful. We can't all be beautiful. And anyway, you can do magic. I don't expect she can."

"No, she can't; she's just a princess. Can't do anything. Totally useless."

"Well, then! Bring her back and show how generous you are."

"It wasn't one of the things I promised,"

muttered Grimwade.

"No, but if you're going to turn over a new leaf," said Gemma, "if you want people to *like* you— "

"Oh, bother!" screamed Grimwade. "A witch isn't allowed any fun at all!"

It had to be said, the beautiful Princess wasn't in the least bit grateful for being brought back. She seemed a rather sulky princess, even though she was so beautiful.

Gemma could understand why Grimwade had taken a dislike to her, but presumably the Prince loved her, or maybe he was just carried away by her incredible beauty.

"So what shall we do now?" said Joel, when the candy floss Princess had gone galumphing off into the trees in search of her Prince.

"What I was thinking – " Ben-Muzzy had gone over to the cauldron and was leaning companionably against it, his head close to Grimwade's. "Seeing as it's All Spells' Night ... how about if we played a trick or two on those Teeny Meanies?"

"Good idea!" sniggered Grimwade. "They need taking down a peg."

"Brilliant!" said Joel. "Let's get started!"

"Hang about," said Gemma. "Isn't it about time we were getting back?"

Joel opened his mouth to protest – and then closed it again. Maybe he'd had enough of playing tricks for one night. The top of his head still felt sore where the hearse had rested on it.

"All right," he said. "I suppose we'd better get back."

"That's a pity," said Ben-Muzzy. "The fun

is just about to begin."

Grimwade tittered.

"I hope you're not going to do anything nasty," said Gemma.

"Us?" said Grimwade.

"After all, there isn't any need, now that you can do your spells properly. Is there?"

Grimwade pulled at a wart on her cheek. "I suppose not," she muttered.

"So let's get going, then." Ben-Muzzy snapped his fingers at the broomstick: it came to him, obediently. "We'll take the twins back first. Jump aboard!"

"I'll go with Grim," said Gemma. "Just to show that I trust her."

Riding with Grimwade was a very different experience from riding with Ben-Muzzy. There were no sudden swoops or lurches as she lost control: no dizzying descents down the air currents, or bumping into cloud banks. And the speed at which she issued her instructions!

"Morf emac ehs erehw ot kcab niwt eht ekat!"

It was like riding on a Rolls-Royce of broomsticks. Gemma didn't feel sick once, not even when they came in to land.

"Thank you," she said. "That was wonderful!"

Grimwade pulled at her wart. "Thanks for teaching me to read," she mumbled.

"That's all right," said Gemma. "I enjoyed it."

There was a swooshing sound, and Joel and Ben-Muzzy arrived. Joel tumbled off. He looked slightly dazed.

"Wow!" he said. "That was fast! Don't they have any speed limits up there?"

"Who cares about speed limits?" cried Ben-Muzzy; and he zoomed upwards again to join Grimwade, who was already circling the trees.

Joel put his hands to his mouth: "KEEP IN TOUCH!"

Ben-Muzzy flapped his cloak as he flew off after Grimwade.

The twins watched for a moment, then slowly turned and walked back down the garden towards the house.

"You know what I went and forgot?" said Gemma. "I forgot to ask her to turn the piranhas back into goldfish. But maybe she'll do it anyway. I think she's happier, now; now that she can read properly. I think she'll turn over a new leaf."

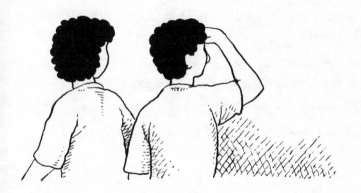

"Oh, yes?" said Joel.

He had shaded his eyes and was looking up. Gemma followed his gaze.

Overhead, a couple of broomsticks were racing side by side. On one of them sat Ben-Muzzy, on the other sat Grimwade. Their heads were close together, their tall steeple hats touching. The sound of sniggering could be heard.

Even as the twins stood watching, Ben-Muzzy and Grimwade vanished and in their places appeared two giant-sized Meanies, complete with horns and pronged tail and a pitchfork. The Meany that was Ben-Muzzy waved its pitchfork in the air; the Meany that was Grimwade swished its tail.

"*Nuf evah ot og ew ffo!*" screeched the Meany that was Grimwade.

Cackling happily, the Wizard and the Witch flew off together into the sunset.

"New leaf?" said Joel.

Gemma sighed. "Well, at least they're friends," she said.